nF418920

The Rise and Fall of Fall of Utopia: An Oral History

Geoffrey Dicker

This book is a work of fiction. Names, characters, places and incidents are either the product of the author's imagination or are used fictitiously. The reader should consult a medical, health or competent professional before adopting any of the suggestions in this book or drawing inferences from it. The author disclaims all responsibility for any liability, loss or risk, personal or otherwise which is incurred as a consequence, directly or indirectly, of the use and application of any of the contents of this book. Any resemblance to actual events, locales or persons, living or dead is purely coincidental.

Cover art by Geoffrey Dicker

Manufactured in the United States of America

ISBN-13: 9798638520472

First Edition

The Rise and Fall of Utopia: An Oral History

Contents

Chapter 1: 10 Days Before the Crisis............................Page 1

Chapter 2: Day 1...Page 22

Chapter 3: Day 7...Page 45

Chapter 4: Day 30...Page 66

Chapter 5: Day 120..Page 96

Chapter 6: Day 365...Page 119

Chapter 7: Year 2...Page 140

Chapter 8: Utopia..Page 157

Chapter 9: Utopia Falls......................................Page 178

Epilogue: ....Page 193

"Don't believe everything you read." - Zen Proverb

"We may have all come in on different ships, but ultimately, we are on the same boat." – Zen Proverb

Chapter 1: 10 Days Before the Crisis.

January 2020 in a universe parallel to ours.

Shawn Cordova, business executive: My friend called me out of the blue and said, "Listen to me. Quit your job immediately. It may sound like crazy talk but hear me out. My friend works for the government. I can't say any more about it. Please trust me. He told me something bad is about to happen very soon. Travel. Eat out. Go to museums. See your friends." I thought he was full of shit. It sounded so ludicrous. Plus, I just got back from a New Year's holiday, so it sounded bizarre to take another trip so soon.

Art Myers, conspiracy theorist: Have you been living under a rock? The signs have always been there for something crazy like this to happen. People are too engrossed in themselves. While we've been making our tiny pittances, the rich have been getting richer. Who's been funding their lavish lifestyles all these years? We have. There have always been opportunities to turn the tables. What has the result been time after time? The people at the top of the pyramid have wielded their power over the masses of people at the bottom who make up the poor. And why? Because too many people accept everything they are told without questioning it or standing up for themselves.

Basil McGee, Vice President of the United States: There were rumors swirling around of impending doom, but for me and my constituents, it's business as usual for conservatives when the House is controlled by liberals. In my daily briefing with President Goodman, I didn't want to alarm him, so I didn't say anything about this. We did talk about what we binge watched over the weekend though. TV shows are so great now. There's this one about politicians who turn out to be reptiles. Hits a little too close to home, but great stuff otherwise!

Shirley Tripp, minimum wage worker: A friend of a friend said something bad was about to happen. I just brushed it off. I have a family to feed and tons of financial obligations.

What am I supposed to do, just drop everything because there is a rumor circulating on the internet? Should we shut down the world because there was a shooting in a major city? I don't believe everything I read. Who has time to read when you're constantly stressed about money?

Tim Francis, priest: One of my pastors told me he'd heard some whispers of a catastrophe headed our way, to the likes of which we have never seen before and we prayed. God always has a plan.

Don Langham, retail store associate: It was business as usual except I noticed people were buying things in bulk. *Why would so many people need 6 pairs of jeans all at once? And what's up with people getting so much coffee and chocolate?* I thought. It was like this day after day. I was wondering if certain people knew something I didn't. I asked some customers and they all gave me very vague answers. Guess they were trying not to start a panic.

Robert Taylor, stockbroker: I got an anonymous tip to dump stock in entertainment ventures and tobacco and invest in stuff like doomsday suits and hand sanitizer. It was the most ludicrous thing I'd ever heard. I may have even gone so far as to tell that person to go to hell.

Brian Garcia, lead singer of The Hands: I don't have time to listen to the news. I'm in a band who has been struggling for years. We've played every shit bar from California to the Jersey Shore. Finally, we had a breakthrough hit. "Touch Me All Over" was becoming a huge smash thanks to our manager getting it placed in a commercial. The band and I pooled all our savings together and we booked our biggest tour ever. We were so excited to play our music to a captive audience.

Jolene Edwards, food blogger & social media influencer: I get paid by restaurants to review their food. My life is fabulous. I'm pretty, I've traveled all over the world for free and eaten such good food at the same time. What's more – people love me! I'm an influencer. Without me, people would not know the difference between fried tarantula and rice cakes. Click and subscribe! While you're at it, smash that like button. I don't watch the news if I am not on it personally. I am too busy to worry about other people's problems.

Shawn Cordova: I came home that night and told my boyfriend about the phone call I received. He said I was crazy. But the thing is, why would my friend lie? Our rational discussion led to a debate. Before long, it escalated to us possibly breaking up over this.

Basil McGee: People overreact over every little thing. This is not a big deal. It'll pass. I needed to clear my head from all these negative headlines. Stressing out only causes wrinkles. I decided to go golfing. But not just to my local golf course. I took a vacation.

Robert Taylor: I didn't want to be accused of insider trading, so I moved a few things around in my portfolio without being too obvious. I didn't tell anyone what I was doing, even though a few people thought I'd lost my mind. Small companies equal poison. Large companies equal gold.

Don Langham: I mean, I work at a mall. Life is not great. I don't get to go to nice restaurants. I can't take luxurious vacations. Sometimes, I don't know how I even scrape enough money together for rent. But I am doing the best I can do. When word got out that people should start stashing dried foods just in case of emergency, I thought, "I can barely afford dinner for tonight, let alone extra food for a possible catastrophe."

Devin Silver, novelist: The world is in a place of despair. Perhaps they need the next great American novel to cheer them up and I'm going to write it for them. I feel this is a calling from God. You know what – I am answering the call. "Hello! This is Devin Silver, at your service."

Marcus Donald, college student: I had deadlines just like always. I'm a great procrastinator, so I did some online shopping as an incentive to get my work done. I never thought anything was wrong until I went online and tried to order some stuff you can normally receive in 24 hours. I was being told there was a 6-8 week wait for those items.

Tim Francis: Our Father who art in Heaven hallowed be thy name. Thy kingdom come; thy will be done on earth as it is in Heaven. Give us this day our daily bread and forgive us our trespasses, as we forgive those who trespass against us. Lead us not into temptation but deliver us from evil. For thine is the kingdom, the power and the glory, forever and ever. Amen.

Brian Garcia: Finally, we were poised for success. It was so exciting to see all those years of hard work finally coming to fruition. My parents were so proud of us for not giving up our dreams and fighting for them.   With such good intentions, what could have possibly gone wrong?

Shawn Cordova: My boyfriend and I got into a shouting match. He started judging the quality of my friends. What a laugh! Did any of his friends try to warn him? I didn't think so.   Finally, we made up. I don't know whether he believed me or not, but at least he backed my decision. We booked a trip to Europe so we could see our friends. Even that turned into a quarrel – "Flight prices are so high," he argued. "Well this could be our last chance, so are you in or out?" I said. He was in.

Basil McGee: Have you ever been to Florida in the wintertime?   It's amazing.   Never too muggy.   The temperature is just perfect. I was here to blow off steam and think about advising my colleagues to do something about this potential crisis. But the reception at the resort was not so great, so I stopped responding to texts after a while.

Art Myers: By the time you are reading these words, it's already too late. I've been trying to warn people for years to turn off the news, conduct your own research from multiple sources and listen to your heart. That's the only way to truly be free.

Shawn Cordova: We were at the airport and I sent my boss a text saying I wouldn't be coming back to the office again. I said he needn't reply and then I shut off my phone. I wish I could have seen his face. He probably had a melt down!

Don Langham: Rumors were starting to spread a few days before things went down that it was going to get crazy busy, so my boss asked me if I wanted to pick up extra shifts. I could always use the money, so of course I said yes.

Jolene Edwards: I have gigs and speaking engagements lined up for almost two years. There's nothing worse in life than empty calendar pages. If no one is paying attention to you, you're irrelevant. If you're not part of the global conversation, you might as well just crawl into a ball and hashtag die.

Art Myers: The global empire exists because the old people are too feeble, and the young people are too stupid.

They should band together but instead all they can do is focus on their generational gap.

Brian Garcia: We were so close to finishing our album. It has multiple bangers on it. We booked studio time while we are out on the road at some of the most prestigious recording studios in history. They cost a pretty penny to reserve, but we know the investment will pay off in spades. The record will come out mid-tour. We definitely have a shot at getting a debut #1 album.

Max Duncan, real estate broker: It's a buyer's market. I've been selling homes for a decade and I've never seen rates this low. I've been making a killing while finding my clients great homes. I did find it strange that apartment sales suddenly became less attractive, and houses outside of the city that seemed to be isolated went up in popularity. The bad news for me is this means I have to take so many trips to the suburbs.

Shawn Cordova: Greece was awesome! Our friends from the UK, Spain and the Netherlands came down to meet us. We partied every night until the sun came up. We spent money like it was going out of style. I didn't want to cause alarm, but I felt I should say something to my friends who'd traveled all the way to join us. That did not go over well at all. I got a lecture about being a conspiracy theorist and was told that I should just keep certain things to myself next time.

Pearl Conway, celebrity: I was at this lavish party at the home of a reality TV star. I won't say who it was, but it got kind of wild. There were no paparazzi around, so we really let loose. By the end of the night, a lot of people were taking drugs and having sex out in the open. It would not surprise me if people got pregnant that night or even worse – contracted sexually transmitted diseases. It was so hedonistic, it bordered on satanic. Who were we to know it would probably be the last time we could do something like that? I probably would have gone even crazier had I known.

Larry Goodman, President of the United States: Don't believe everything you hear. There is nothing to worry about. My administration and I have everything under control. If you've heard the rumors that are circulating and are concerned about catching something, wear a body suit and don't be a disgusting pig. Like I said, we are not saying there is anything wrong, but I can tell you with 100% certainty, if you use sanitizer, you can kill whatever this thing is or isn't. I've heard smokers are more susceptible to whatever this rumor is.

Mary Keaton, leading hand sanitizer brand CEO: Our stock started going through the roof. Out of nowhere. The president makes one speech and suddenly stores can't keep it in stock. For years, we sold at $6 per share and then it went to $10. Then $12. Then $18. Then it started doubling and tripling within a matter of days. It was crazy. But it's great for business so I had nothing to complain about. I felt bad for cigarette manufacturers. Their stocks plummeted.

Steven Cooke, patient zero: A couple of weeks ago, I woke up as normal and when I went to pee for the first time that morning, it felt like Satan was coming out of my dick. I don't want to get too graphic, but it was one of the most painful things I've ever experienced. I waited a couple of hours and there was no change, so I thought I'd better go to the hospital right away. The doctors said they'd never seen anything like it. My cock turned red and swelled up huge. I could barely tuck it in my pants. I was scared to drink anything for fear I'd have to pee again.

Shawn Cordova: Me and the boyfriend quit smoking many years ago. But since we were living it up in Europe, we figured why the hell not? This trip was a non-stop party. I think we were each going through a pack a day. After a couple of days, I noticed he started coughing a lot. I didn't think anything of it because of the smoking. It was probably just that his lungs weren't used to it anymore.

Franco Tybalt, pet shop owner: I've owned Boys Pet Shop for close to twenty years. Sometimes right before a rainstorm or an earthquake, you'll see a few of the animals freak out a little bit. But this was like nothing I've ever experienced before. There was a screaming sound I will never forget as long as I live. It was like the animals were begging to be let out of their cages. I talked to a few of my colleagues in the industry who also run pet stores. They were all saying the same thing.

Florence Cox, day care worker: Pancake Thursday is everyone's favorite day of the month. I bring in all the fixins for the children to have a delicious and semi-unhealthy breakfast. As toppings, we had fruit, chocolate, whipped cream, you name it. Naturally, with all the sugar they just consumed, I expected the kids to be a little jumpy, but this was out of control. They were unruly. They were acting like it was the last time they were ever going to play. I had to call each parent and tell them to get their kid. I just couldn't control them.

Art Myers: Well this is a no brainer. You've got a conservative guy in office who's brainwashed the old people into believing what he says. The younger generation of liberals hate him and think he's full of shit. How could there not be some political friction? He who shouts the loudest usually wins.

Frankie Palmer, police force: There was this unspoken tension in the air, some say it was because the country was divided. But even so, crime seemed to be on a downward cycle. We've had meetings to discuss laying off some of the force. Petty crime will probably never change, but for the first time since I've been a cop, there was not a spike in major crime like murder.

Debra Curtis, grocery store clerk: It's like the world started to change between Monday and Friday. It was business as usual at first but then suddenly we had a hard time keeping anything in stock. Coffee and candy bars became impossible to get. All the stores were out of it too. Condoms were all gone, but everyone stopped buying cigarettes. It was odd. Was there some sort of joke we were not privy to?

Shane Gross, conservative news media: The liberals are trying to cause anxiety by panic buying up all the condoms and coffee and candy bars. What do they think this is going to do? Impeach the president? Keep trying liberals. You're all a bunch of idiots.

Jeff Richards, liberal news media: Rumors of a virus that is causing men's dicks to burn when they pee are starting to spread, no pun intended, after a man was rushed to the hospital saying the devil was trying to escape from his cock. There are no other details at this time, but we will keep monitoring the story. We can say with certainty it was probably caused by a dirty conservative, who was in denial about their cleanliness.

Tim Francis: Come on. Satan inside a man's genitals? People think my congregation are whack jobs for believing in our lord and savior Jesus Christ. I will continue to follow the practices of our lord and savior Jesus Christ. I encourage you to do the same. Amen.

Nick Hopkins, stock market investor: Hot damn! I made $3 million in just about a week from investing in coffee, body suits and hand sanitizer. I dumped all my tobacco investments. I have a separate bank account from my wife, otherwise I would love to tell her about my windfall. But what I will do is get her a diamond necklace or something nice. I'm gonna look like a hero!

Brian Garcia: When we hit the road, our bass player kept saying stupid shit like, "What if the van crashes and we all die before we become bona fide superstars?" Now why would anyone want to put that energy out into the world? The first show was a sellout. The crowd lost their minds. Dare I say it was our best gig ever.

Jeff Richards: People should stay away from large groups, including orgies and try and refrain from having sex and touching yourself. There are reports coming in from all over the world people's genitals are swelling up and whatever this is is very painful. If you need to be out in public, try not to sit down on anything and don't rub your body parts on any public surface. If you've got body suits, it would be a good idea to wear them as an extra layer of protection. Sorry to those of you in warmer climates.

Steven Cooke: I thought after a couple of days on antibiotics, things were going to get better. It didn't. It spread to my ass and it burned to put any pressure against my crotch area. I couldn't lay down, so I just stood in the hospital pacing back and forth hoping for some relief. I didn't get any.

Rachel Morgan, college student: I have some sick friends. There was a video circulating of a guy who had this really inflamed dick. It was kind of disgusting looking, but like a train wreck, I couldn't look away. The quality of the video was not great, like a hidden camera inside a hospital. Within a few days, the whole university had either seen it or heard about it. I hate to use the term, but it went viral.

Devin Silver: The question was, what would I write about? Politics are so boring. Everyone talks about that. We already have our masters who have perfected the genres of science fiction, horror and fantasy. I need to get to the heart of what America has on its mind and explore the subject.   Though I don't have anything concrete, I know I am just around the corner from having a breakthrough.

Virgil Moss, psychic: I am seeing something unusual. It's like the end of sex. I can't explain. People just won't touch themselves or each other anymore.   Humanity is in jeopardy. People will die. A lot of people. Before they do, it's going to be very painful. When the survivors emerge, the world is going to be a different place than it is today.

Debra Curtis: My manager called me aside and said we should not put out our entire stock of certain products to save some for others.   Whatever we did put out, sold out as fast as we could put it on the shelves. It was very strange to say the least.

Shawn Cordova: We hadn't been fooling around that much because our days were long, partying and hanging with friends. We went to a strip club and I found it really strange that my boyfriend was rubbing money all over his genitals before giving it to strippers, but to each his own. I didn't want a trip to Europe to pass without having hot sex. When I started touching my boyfriend, he recoiled in horror. I thought he might have been cheating on me, but we were together the whole time. If he was that stealth, I figured I deserved it.

Steven Cooke: Doctors of all kinds were coming in all the time. Then government officials wanted to talk to me as well. They asked what I'd been doing, where I'd been, if I had any contact with other people. That kind of stuff. I had nothing to hide. I didn't do anything wrong. I just wanted to sleep. My boss had recently gotten back from Vegas and won a shit load of money. He gave me a $10,000 bonus for being loyal. I did what I thought anyone who received a windfall would do.   I took all my clothes off and rolled around in it for a few hours.

Greg Fisher, strip club owner: This guy comes in and just starts handing out cash to people. I work at a strip club by the airport where we get tourists from all over the world, so I am used to seeing all kinds of crazy shit, but it was quite odd. All the tittie dancers said this guy gave each of them $500 that he stuffed down their G-strings that night. Then a few days later, all my girls called in sick. If this was some ploy for all of them to get a raise, I didn't find it funny at all. I had to close the club down because I had no dancers. I told them if they don't get their asses back to work immediately, they are fired. They showed up alright. Everything went back to normal and then a few days later, people were calling up the club and asking me why their private parts were burning. When the first few people called, I thought it was a weird coincidence. Then my phone started ringing off the hook. *Oh shit*, I thought.

Chapter 2: Day 1

Dolores Pena, mainstream media: Breaking news. We are getting reports from multiple cities that people's crotches are on fire. We realize it sounds funny, but it's apparently no laughing matter. This story is developing.

Shawn Cordova, business executive: We got back from Greece and my boyfriend was doubled over in pain. I took him to Urgent Care. They said we probably just had some gnarly butt sex and everything should return to normal in a day or two. It was probably an STD so they gave him some antibiotics. Pisses me off. He must have been cheating on me. It got worse as the day went on. I tried to tell him to wait for the drugs to kick in, but I could tell by the look on his face he was serious. I rushed him to the hospital.

Heidi Day, hospital worker: A virus is starting to circulate around the world that is affecting the ass, cock and pussy hole. As such we are calling it ACPh6.9 for short. If someone has a snazzier title, please reach out to us immediately. We're having our art department design a graphic, so time is of the essence. Anyway, due to this mysterious little bugger, we are asking for people to stay home and only leave your house for important things just until we figure out what is happening. This is not officially approved by the government, but we'd hate to be in a position after it's too late where we have to say, "You should have listened to us."

Liam Waters, college student: Fuck this staying home crap! I'm 21 years old and I've been looking forward to spring break all semester. I can get as drunk as I want and bang as many hot chicks as there are hours in the day. If you think I am obeying the rules, you don't even know how wrong you are.

Frankie Atkins, introvert: I have been waiting for this moment my whole life! I hate going out. People are just mean and cruel, and I don't like leaving my house if I can avoid it. This is pretty much my dream come true. Welcome to my world, everyone!

Anthony Gibson, office worker: They want us to stay in and work from home? This is the best news ever. My boss is so busy he usually only has time to drop by my desk in between meetings and dump a pile of work on me. Out of sight out of mind. This is going to be like getting free money.

Cara Wilkerson, hospital chief of staff: We'd like to loosen the guideline to allow "essential workers" to be able to still work. This includes hospitals and food professionals. Non-essential workers include the entertainment industry, ball players, teachers and prostitutes. If your industry was not listed, it's probably not essential. We ask for your compliance. You can use this time to find something meaningful to do with your life.

Carole Diaz, prostitute: How am I supposed to work from home? Call my clients on video and tell them to fuck themselves?

Ralph Morgan, fast food associate: So I am supposed to risk my life and be exposed to sick people for barely over minimum wage? Something is very fishy here. I am not just saying that because I work at a take-out seafood restaurant.

Art Myers, conspiracy theorist: Wait until they call the national guard out to quote unquote protect us. As soon as it happens, our rights are going to start getting taken away one by one. They are going to make people think they are unsafe with the misinformation they spew out through our TVs. It's called programming for a reason. People are going to be begging to be protected. We are walking right into their trap.

Brian Garcia, lead singer of The Hands: We were three days into our tour. It was like each new day was the best day of my life. It sounds cheesy but sometimes dreams really come true. On the fourth day of the tour, we'd just rolled into Memphis. Our manager told us the show might be canceled. What could have gone wrong? Low ticket sales? Something else? It was none of those things our manager assured us. There was some sort of virus spreading around various cities. People were just trying to take precautions. Fuck the precautions. We just wanna rock!

Jolene Edwards, food blogger & social media influencer: What an inconvenience! Several of my engagements got canceled. I had the flights booked and everything. I have a lot of power and I advised the clients I would be sure to tell all my followers about this. They all profusely apologized and said it was out of their control, but I took it personally. That's not how you treat a star!

Virgil Moss, psychic: The world is on fire. That's what the spirit guides are telling me. It's not a literal fire, but a metaphorical one. No one is safe. Lots of changes are coming. It's about to be activated. If you want a full reading, you're going to have to pay up. I can't give everything away.

Tim Francis, priest: Homosexuality is sin. Plain and simple. The bible doesn't say it literally, but no one can understand Shakespeare so what makes you think people would get something supposedly written before then. God speaks in metaphors. I talk to God often and he doesn't like the gays. This is punishment for their evil ways. We all have to suffer for it. I pray it'll take them first. Sinners!

Darin Bones, gay rights activist: Oh, fuck that religious guy! In the ass! He probably enjoys it anyway. They are just a bunch of bible beaters trying to fool the weak minded. No one knows where this came from, but I can assure you gays are a peace-loving people with amazing fashion sense. Stop listening to these religious freak-a-zoids. All they are doing is trying to divide us. God loves all people. It actually says that in the bible unlike the hateful bullshit they are spewing!

Debra Curtis, grocery store clerk: Officially, something is up in the world. I don't know what it is. It's like people are binge hoarding everything. We're going to have to hire more people if this keeps up. They are telling people unofficially to stay home, then everyone is complaining about it. Now everyone is mad. I don't know what's really going on. There's so much misinformation. Are we supposed to stay home or not? Are we safe or not?

Neil Wong, mainstream media: We still don't know more about the mysterious crotch inflammations being reported in multiple cities, but we are expecting a press conference from the president any minute now. He should be explaining this more in detail. We would like to preface his speech by saying almost everything that comes out of his mouth is pure and utter bullshit, so we'd like to remind everyone to be advised.

Larry Goodman, President of the United States: There is no CrotchVirus! This is a hoax to try and oust me from power. Do not believe anything you hear coming out of those fat liberal mouths. I'm the president! Would I lie to you? Before you try to answer, it's rhetorical. I've been amazing to my people so far and I will continue to be amazing. If you're really afraid of this thing, wash your entire body with hand sanitizer. Wear a body suit underneath. It might not smell very good after you've worn it all day, but it's the best protection there is on the market. Live your lives as normal! Have sex! Eat out. Just take the normal precautions you always would. Use condoms. Stay away from spicy food and dangerous neighborhoods.

Michael Hunt, reporter: Mr. President, should we stay at home during all this? We've been hearing that on the news.

Larry Goodman: The news is fake. You're a fake. I am the real deal. Put your trust in me. I'm taking a brief little vacation and then I'll give another press conference.

Devin Silver, novelist: Now this sounds kind of silly, but there's all this talk on the news of a CrotchVirus. It's mostly rumors at this point, but it seems like an interesting story. Such conflicting information too. What if this thing was true? It would be bigger than race. It would be grander than religion because it affects everyone. Now that's a story! I'm going to keep taking notes and monitoring the situation. This could be just what I'm looking for.

Shane Gross, conservative news media: You heard it from the president's own lips. There is no CrotchVirus. ACPh6.9 is a hoax. He has advised us to continue to live life normally. In fact, he encouraged us all to go out to our favorite establishments owned by conservatives, have a cocktail or two to blow off some steam and stimulate the economy.

Jeff Richards, liberal news media: Seems a few places are considering shutting down for a few days as rumors of the CrotchVirus, as they are calling it, are spreading. The president has advised business as normal, but we all know he's an ass hat and should not be trusted under any circumstances.

Steven Cooke, patient zero: I am getting really tired of all these jerks from the government trying to man-whore shame me. Yes. I slept with prostitutes and strippers that night. I'm a horny guy. Why are people holding it against me? I can tell you what, if this pain doesn't start to subside, I am going to commit suicide. I can't take it much longer. It hurts to walk. It hurts to sit. It hurts to stand. It's on my ass and my dick. I've lost so much weight. I can't eat or drink. When I do, the pain to expel it is unbearable.

Ira Noonan, liberal: Going to family gatherings has become painful. All we do is get into arguments over politics. We were making so much social progress in the world and now it seems like there's a dark cloud over everything making people argue with their loved ones over their beliefs. Neither side is wrong for believing what they think is right, but in the grand scheme of things, we can't do anything to change it. Do they know this?

Joshua Noonan, Ira's father: Kids get their feelings hurt over everything nowadays. My son tells me to stop watching the conservative news. Why? They've got these sexy women who poke holes in his liberal views. The truth hurts. He recites all these so-called facts and none of them were discussed on the programs I watch. How could that be? I'm older and wiser and I don't think he knows what he's talking about.

Art Myers: The media is making you divert your attention while bad things are happening behind the scenes. Mark my words. I think the government, or some cartel of evil is responsible for this. If we knew all the things they've kept hidden from us, there would be a revolution. People would not be that stupid to just sit back and do nothing. Granted, it's happened so many times throughout history, it's almost embarrassing. We trusted them and they took advantage of us.

Liam Waters, college student: We keep hearing school might close for a few weeks! Hip Hip Hooray! I am so behind in my studies anyway. They are saying it has to do with that video of the guy with the swollen cock. The power of social media. We all shared it around the college. Now people all over the world have seen it. Never underestimate students. I hope they will cancel all the debt we're in too, but somehow, I think it's a pipedream.

Geri Burton, airline stewardess: The president has suggested we cleanse everything to stop this panic from spreading so now we have to wash down all seats and equipment before passengers get on board. What an aggravation! I liked things better the way they were before. People sat in filth for decades and no one got sick. This is just a nasty rumor trying to make us work harder for no additional pay.

Barbara Higgins, entrepreneur: In all periods of history, there is someone who comes up with a genius idea out of nowhere. Mine is organic hand sanitizer called "OrgoSani." It's just water in a fancy bottle. In our defense, no animals were harmed in the manufacturing process. I had been hearing stores can't keep this shit in stock, so I might as well capitalize on people's stupidity. It's the

American way, after all. We're selling out of it like... well, like water!

Steven Cooke: Fuck it I'm going to jump out of the window.

Dolores Pena, mainstream media: We are getting reports the world's first victim of the CrotchVirus has passed away. They say he committed suicide, but it's being treated as an ACPh6.9 death. We will continue to monitor this story and keep you updated.

Jolene Edwards: At least now I have some answers. My events are being canceled because people are afraid of some crotch thing. I don't see what it has to do with me. People still need to eat at fancy restaurants. People still need to know what luxury food is hot and what is not. Just wash your hands and don't touch your genitals after you eat. I think this has been blown way out of proportion.

Larry Goodman: Use your cash and get hand sanitizer. I want to reiterate, there is no need to panic. However, if I were you, I'd go to the store today.

Debra Curtis: The lines were miles long. We can't keep anything in stock. Everyone says we are all in this together, yet I saw young people pushing old people out of the way to get supplies. Ironic since everyone seems to have forgotten their food allergies in times like this. I just don't get why EVERYTHING is selling out. It's like people wanted to have something to show for waiting in lines up to 3 hours long. Well enjoy that package of diapers even though you don't have any kids. People are too much sometimes!

Jimmy Rios, mainstream media: This just in. The world has identified the first female victim of this possibly deadly CrotchVirus. All we know is she is a porn star and her breasts are pretty gigantic.

Arabella Pope, patient zero: First my pussy was on fire. Then it spread to my ass. I was hoping it was complications from my massive breast implants, but it's not. I hate this. I thought I could screw the pain away, so I filmed an unprotected sex gang bang last night. Lots of porn stars from all over the world were there. A few people started experiencing a burning dick sensation right after shooting ended. I didn't say anything.

Frankie Palmer, police force: As of now, everything is under control. Please stay orderly. Please don't be selfish douches. We have a lot of elderly people. Though we don't expect them to live long, they should still have access to the things everyone else has.

Tim Francis: God will take care of all of this for us. Put your faith in God and keep praying. Straight people, we will get through this. Gays, this is your punishment for centuries of sinning.

Darin Bones: Hey Father Francis, I talked to God last night. She asked me to tell you to please walk outside without gloves or a body suit, touch a sick person, go home that night and pray. Let us know how it all works out for you. It would be preferred if it's not a young boy for a change.

Franco Tybalt, pet shop owner: They are dying! A bunch of pets are dropping dead out of nowhere. What is causing this? I don't understand. The shrieking noises they make before expiring are the worst sounds I've ever heard. I wish someone could tell us what is going on.   You don't even want to know about the smell.

Larry Goodman: There is no CrotchVirus in all countries. Do not panic. I'm doing an amazing job. How does my suit look? Dope, right?

Jimmy Rios: President Goodman says there is no CrotchVirus.

Walter Burns, concerned citizen: Goodman said there is no CrotchVirus in all countries and the news took his quote out of context! Can't they get fined for that?

Shawn Cordova: My boyfriend has been quarantined. This is scary. I dropped him off at the hospital and they said I can visit through a glass wall any time I want. It's like a glory hole, except no one is getting off. It's making me wonder if the only thing we had in our relationship was sex. This is going to sound crappy, but I am considering breaking up with him.

Danny Clay, disease control specialist: At the moment, there are a lot of unclear things about ACPh6.9. We don't know very much about this as the virus is so new, so we asked philanthropist Ozzie Madden his advice because he's donated millions of dollars to our organization. We know for sure it spreads through human contact and from touching your genitals. Most likely, the entire money supply is tainted also. We are developing testing as we speak. It's called a Crotch Blocker and looks like a dildo. The bad news is we have to stick it up your ass and move it back and forth aggressively for about 2 minutes. It's really painful too. Results have been inconclusive so far. We hope the testing kit keeps getting better and better.

Art Myers: How come they are so definite about certain things related to ACPh6.9, yet they are so vague about other parts of it?   Control.   Someone at the top of the pyramid knows what this is. Probably not the president because he's a shithead and schmuck. Why would doctors be taking medical advice from a philanthropist? I think they are pumping us full of fear and disseminating conflicting information, so we don't know what's real and what isn't. How come grocery store clerks can work, but we can't go to our offices? Do they have special powers the rest of us don't have? Some of the things they are saying sound ludicrous, but who wants to risk it, just in case they are true? None of this adds up. They might as well just get it out of the way and tell us that aliens are really in control of the world and are pulling all the strings just to really confuse the hell out of people.

Shawn Cordova: They are doing testing where they ram something up people's asses? I am going to consider it cheating on me, so I can break up with my boyfriend on a technicality. Then I won't feel so bad about this situation.

It's unfortunate, but what else am I supposed to do? Risk my health each day to go see someone who's most likely as good as dead?

Damien Campos, anti-vaxxer: A vaccine? Please! I have been eating organic my entire life. I don't want their stupid vaccine. It's probably poison anyway. Nothing is going up my ass except a nice hard cock! From someone who eats healthy, of course.

Terry Reynolds, pandemic comedian: I have done my stand-up act in Kansas City, LA and Las Vegas, but I just didn't seem to cross over into the mainstream. I amassed a lot of social media followers, so I am just going to do my act there, one line at a time. Can't hurt anything, right? If this thing is truly real, there's going to be a lot of sad people. I will spread joy to those in need. If I can make at least one person smile, it was all worth it. Also, I am unemployed as fuck. What else have I got to do?

Florence Cox, children's daycare worker: I've been in touch with the parents of my children. Nothing is getting better. The kids are unruly.   We will not take them back if we cannot get a handle on this situation. In the meanwhile, my staff and I are just sitting around taking long lunches, maybe having a cocktail or two in the office.   If this continues, we might need to shutter our doors. Come on parents! Do your job and control your monsters!

Casey Sanchez, college student: All the students are sending emails to the professors saying they cannot complete their assignments on time because they are too afraid to come to class. It's working! We've been getting extensions. The students are out powering the teachers. This is unprecedented.   Maybe we can have them cancel exams and finals! We will risk it to attend graduation and frat parties though. Just can't tell them. Don't sell us out, oldsters!

Brian Garcia: We had a band meeting. The manager told us we should be prepared to take a week off. It's a disappointment, but on an up note, we might be able to take in some sight-seeing.   Usually when we go to these cities, we see whatever we can from the tour van. Then we crash out, go to the gig, practice all day, play the show, screw hot chicks, pass the hell out and head to the next city.

Shirley Tripp, minimum wage worker: When I was warned to take some time off and stash a few things away, I should have listened. The lines for the grocery store are very long and the prices of everything have gone up. I couldn't afford life before. Now it's worse. I don't know what I am going to do!

Jolene Edwards: The worst thing ever has happened. I had to eat at home last night.   What the hell do I know about cooking?   I couldn't risk getting caught ordering take out. What if they put me on a list of common people? This will blow over. When it does, I am not going to show any mercy to those people who canceled on me.

Art Myers: Are you a lemming? It's so obvious what is going on. Most people are not going to take the time to fact check so the news can get away with saying anything and people will believe it. All the president talks about is how wonderful he is? Come on!   Ever been to a party where you meet one of these egotists? They act like they are so great, but they are hiding something. People who have nothing to hide are completely transparent.

Terry Reynolds: Now when you're a sick fuck, you're really a sick fuck. There's no need to panic, we have a total lunatic in charge telling us to keep calm. Maybe less is more?

Nick Hopkins, stockbroker: Moderation was never my strong suit. When you're up, you're up. The stock market like everything else is addictive especially when you're on a hot streak. The tough part is knowing when to quit. It reminds me of snorting cocaine. You promise yourself you are going to stop and you can do it at any time, but deep down, you know you can't.

Kacey Davenport, state governor: Mr. President, we are begging you. Please take this seriously. This is our chance to meet the moment and get ahead of this before it gets out of control.

Larry Goodman: Nothing and no one will control me. Especially not some invisible monster virus.

Chapter 3: Day 7

Cara Wilkerson, hospital chief of staff: If anyone tries to tell you this is not a global emergency, they are full of shit. The number of cases is escalating exponentially every day. Hospitals all over the globe are out of beds for new patients. We will run out of supplies and resources if this doesn't slow down soon. Please take this seriously. Stay away from people. Stop having sexy time, right now! Self-isolate not just for your safety, but for the safety of others.

Larry Goodman, President of the United States: There is no emergency. Do not panic. My team and I have got a handle on this liberal virus. We are working with local governments all over the world. I want you all to know I'll be canceling the vacation I was supposed to take this week so that I can continue to monitor the situation. I know what you're thinking – this must be a huge inconvenience for me. It is. If you feel safer, stay home. Just because a doctor suggests it, doesn't make it true. Who's in charge? Me or science? We both know the answer. Please continue to use hand sanitizer. It works. In fact, there is a fresh supply being shipped in from overseas. Whatever you do, don't believe what you're hearing on the liberal news. It's a smear campaign to make me look bad. Put your trust in me. Have I ever lied before?

Art Myers, conspiracy theorist: The president is suggesting using hand sanitizer. He's always wrong and lies, so I am not going to follow anything he says. Take what I am saying with a grain of salt. I am not trying to worry people. I'm not suggesting any medical advice since I am not a doctor. He is the one doing it. Based on his past mistruths, this is what scares me.

Dolores Pena, mainstream media: 1,000 deaths have been reported globally with a possible 10,000 infected with the CrotchVirus aka the invisible monster enemy aka ACPh6.9. The president is telling people not to panic. We are not trying to cause any alarms, but we are a little worried and here's why you should be worried too: the numbers seem to be going up. Way up and not down.

There are reports that people are flocking to stores and hoarding food and other supplies. There is a lot of uncertainty in the air.

Shane Gross, conservative news media: We don't need to focus on containing this rumored virus. Instead, we should spend all our energy blaming the liberals. I repeat – that is the most useful thing you can do at this time. As soon as you've exhausted all your energy from that, please go to the stores and panic buy. Buy guns if necessary to make sure you feel safe. All rules are out the window. Push and shove elderly liberals out of the way so you can provide for your family.

Art Myers: Well that's convenient. Now that this is already out of control, they want to put us in lockdown. They are going to fuck everything up in private while people are not on the streets. When we are finally released from self-quarantine, I'll bet everything turns to shit, if it hasn't already. This is the way they designed it. They don't want us to succeed. This system is beyond broken. It was set up in a way that will never allow us to get ahead. It couldn't be any more obvious than it is now. Wake up people!

Franco Tybalt, pet shop owner: Animals across the world are dying off in droves. The ones that are still alive are pissed! They can carry the virus and give it to you. By the desperation in their faces, they will. I am an animal lover and I hate to suggest this, but trust me, for your safety and the safety of others, lock them up!

Terry Reynolds, pandemic comedian: Your CrotchVirus name calculator is your first name plus your last name. That's also your quarantine name and your porn star name!

Ozzie Madden, philanthropist: We are working to combat this invisible monster disease.   A virus similar to this was made in a lab by a company that I have a major stake in, but it seems to have mutated. People question why we are spending so much energy on testing instead of a cure. Because we need to have proper numbers to give to the news media so it justifies your lockdown orders. Besides, if you don't get tested, how will you know for sure if you have it? Once a test has been created, rich people and celebrities will have access first. We must protect them. All lives matter, but their lives matter more. I'm not only a billionaire, but I'm friends with a lot of famous people as well as the president and they all trust me. Maybe you should too?

Dolores Pena: As the rules for lockdown are being established, you are being asked to stand at least 10 feet apart from other people to make sure your cooties don't spread. It's ok to risk it at grocery stores, but not at public parks. Say it with me: grocery stores good, parks bad. The president has no comment on this.

Art Myers: If we maintain the safety distance and take the necessary precautions that the news is recommending, what's the difference between going to a grocery store or the beach? Nothing. You know why one is ok but not the other? To have power over us. No one knows what is really

happening. If they do, they are not letting us in on the gag.
I am very suspect.

Victor Carter, stockbroker: What a roller coaster! Every
time the president speaks, the market is up and down
faster than a hooker in a hotel room with a married man.
What I can tell you is you probably already missed the boat
on getting hand sanitizer at a cheap rate, but if I were you,
I'd dump all your other stocks and get as much as you can.
It's better than gold!

Tim Francis, priest: We are continuing to pray. We are
very confident God and Jesus have heard our prayers and
will be answering them soon. To everyone out there,
please continue to get down on your knees as much as
possible during this trying time.

Cara Wilkerson: Our team has been working non-stop
since this outbreak began. We are severely understaffed.
We're trying to keep the public safe, so we've mandated
that every member of our organization work without

taking any time off. If you get caught napping in the break room, consider yourself looking for a new job.   Also, we recommend people wear Hazmat suits whenever possible, but since there are not enough to go around, take everything you've got in your closet and wear it all at the same time.   It will probably not protect you, but it might get you some social media attention if you post photos of it since soon, none of us will be allowed to do anything fun.

George Foster, social media enthusiast: Suddenly everyone's an expert on every topic. People that I've known online for years, who rarely chat with me are coming out of the woodwork to slam my ideas. I've blocked family members and I am saddened to find out how selfish people are in times of crisis. Why are my so-called friends posting selfies while people are dying? Social media is a cesspool of the worst in humanity. It's not even fun to go online anymore, but there's nothing else to do!

Brian Garcia, lead singer of The Hands: Our tour got put on permanent hold. What are we going to do?   This was our life savings. We are getting hate mail from fans saying that they will never buy our music again because the ticket agency is refusing to refund people's money. They changed their terms and conditions to say that no refunds will be made because the tour will get rescheduled eventually. It's not going to happen. We don't have any more money. The venues, hotels and airlines are not refunding our booking fees, so we don't know what to do. We might have to resort to busking on the streets, but I am being told even that is not safe because we are not supposed to be out in public. This is an utter disaster and public relations nightmare.

Devin Silver, novelist: I've got it! I'll write about this so-called CrotchVirus.   I know there will be a lot of information out there, but I am sure I can use my skills to come up with a perspective that no one has ever heard before. Hopefully other writers will think the market is flooded with virus stories, so they write about something else.

Joe Buchanan, supermarket CEO: Despite what you might be hearing on the news, there is not a food shortage. I repeat - we are not running out of food. What we are running out of; however, is workers who give a shit enough to keep your groceries safe.

Virgil Moss, psychic: This is a trying time where lots of misinformation will be spreading. People will be choosing sides. Power shifts and role reversals will be happening. Stay vigilant. Stay awake. Stay safe. Stay home. Stay sexy.

Shawn Cordova, business executive: It's not looking so good for my boyfriend.   The hospital keeps calling me to ask if I want to see him one more time before it's too late. I choose to remember him the way he once was. Besides, going to a hospital is like going into the belly of the beast. I am not going to do that, especially since his chances for survival are so low. I'll text him later. Maybe I'll even send a dick pic so he can remember the good old days.

Debra Curtis, grocery store clerk: This is some serious ass bullshit. We are working our butts off for minimum wage! I haven't had a day off since this started. Every time I go home to my family, I risk getting them sick since I've been exposed to these diseased people all day long. We are firefighters on the front lines and being treated like second class citizens. I told my boss how ridiculous this was, and the guy gave me a certificate because he donated money to charity in my name. What the hell am I supposed to do with that? Wipe my ass?   Well, I might have to since all these morons panicked and bought up all the damned toilet paper!

Joseph Simpson, hotelier: The hospitality industry has officially turned to shit overnight. Everyone is canceling their trips. Business looks bleak for the immediate future. We've got all kinds of food that is going to go bad. All sorts of contracts we cannot back out of. I know we are not the only ones going through this but if things don't change and very soon, we are absolutely screwed!

Esteban Villanueva, mortician: Business is booming. Unfortunately, it means people are dying. As soon as we dig one grave, another body comes in. I hate to be gross, but their private parts are so swollen and red. It's nasty. We don't really know what the origin of this sickness was, but it looks very painful. Imagine not being able to pee or poop! It does not sound very good at all.

Dan Hutson, real estate broker: Well this is fucked. We thought people would be panic buying homes, but it seems everyone is too uncertain about what is going on, so everything is on hold. Interest rates are in the toilet. The market is tanking. Condo sales are almost completely off the table right now because people don't want to live near anyone.

Florence Cox, day care professional: This is not affecting kids like it affects adults. Their genitals are not on fire. Instead, they don't stop vomiting. If you go into any classroom in the world without a gas mask, you'll throw-up from the smell of puke. It's not their fault. They can't help it, but at the same rate, it's disgusting. We're going to have to cancel school all together if this doesn't change soon. Calling a parent to tell them their child has died is the worst phone call to ever have to make.

Terry Reynolds: Some people like to pray before bed. I like to say, "This has been another episode of the Twilight Zone."

Larry Goodman: The liberal media can go to hell. Why are people panicking? There's less than 1,000 people around the world that have died from this. We've had wars where there've been more casualties. No one freaked out over that. Everyone just calm down. People are calling for lockdown and I am demanding for business to resume as normal. And they wonder why this country is divided. Because no one listens to me! Who's in charge? Not you!

Sarah Cole, small business owner: To stop the further spread of this CrotchVirus, we are asking our non-essential workers to stay home. Unfortunately, it goes against the wishes of the White House, so we will not get any funding. It also means we are going to have to lay off a ton of workers. We just want to protect the masses at large. We appreciate your patience and hope you'll comply with what the government tells us.

Larry Goodman: The CrotchVirus, which was most likely started by the liberals, is spreading rapidly throughout the world. People are dying. Also children and pets are extremely vulnerable. We might have to euthanize them all for the safety of the world. We are in talks to impose a "non-essential worker" clause whereby if your job is not absolutely crucial to the betterment of the economy, you are being asked to stay home. Celebrities and sports figures, please sit down and shut up. This is going to cause massive unemployment. The stock market is going to crash and burn which will probably lead to riots, murders and martial law, but we must do this to protect the masses at large. Please try to be part of the solution and not part of the problem. This is a trying time for all of us and especially the liberals who got us into this mess. I want to close by saying, none of this is my fault.

Jeff Richards, liberal news media: The president finally admits there's a problem and all he can do is try and place blame. This is the time to step up, rise to the challenge and solve problems. On behalf of everyone in our country, we would like to apologize for having such a crappy leader.

Amos Palumbo, airline steward: President Goodman makes one speech and the entire country shuts down. It took nearly 14 hours for a normal 5-hour trip because every flight was getting canceled. The airports are deserted, and planes are empty. People don't want to risk sitting down because they aren't sure if the virus can live on seats and everyone is out of hand sanitizer. That's another thing that pisses me off. Since I am hashtag venting – how come hand sanitizer is the closest thing we have to a cure, yet you can't get it anywhere? If they really cared about us, they would find a way to get it to everyone. People are acting as if eye contact spreads the virus. For all we know, it does. Every day, it seems to change.

Brian Garcia: Before you spend all your money on trying to save yourselves and your families, could you please donate to our campaign?   We are $200,000 short and we could really use your help. We are going to live stream concerts from our kitchen because the only thing we are good at is being musicians. This is kind of a shitty time to learn our chosen professions are non-essential in making the world turn. Hey. That's a great idea for a song!

Terry Reynolds: I've tested positive for being totally over this shit! I have all the symptoms for being absolutely hilarious.

Cara Wilkerson: Effective immediately, unprotected masturbation is banned. If you do need to touch yourself, please wear gloves or use hand sanitizer to completely wash your genitals. We are also asking people to not show up at hospitals if they think they just have a normal STD.

We are overloaded with new patients. We really need to reserve these hospital beds for true emergencies.

Lenny Curtis, condom manufacturer: Sales of condoms have gone through the roof. There's a lot of misinformation out there. People think putting a condom on your penis is going to protect you from this virus. Granted, we have no proof either way at this point, so we are just going to sit back and celebrate that our company is not going to go out of business for the foreseeable future.

Nick Hopkins, stock market investor: Every time a press conference happens, the stock market plummets. If this keeps up, there's going to be a complete collapse. Shit! It just went down again. I think it's time to do something I never do, especially in sex – pull out! I made and lost 10 million dollars in less than 2 weeks.

Dolores Pena: After a representative from the stock market told people not to panic, everyone started to panic. Stocks took a huge tumble. There is chaos everywhere.

Larry Goodman: Use hand sanitizer. We've got plenty now. Lather yourselves up everywhere. Even down there.

Shawn Cordova: I am doing the exact opposite of what the president says. It's called hand sanitizer, not dick sanitizer bird brain! I don't understand that guy. He's not a doctor. All he does is lie and make shit up. But I truly don't know what to do. All I can say is I don't trust him. I'm telling all my friends to do the same. Over the phone, of course, since we are not supposed to see each other.

Neil Wong: Over 1,500 people reported dead. An estimated 20,000 people are infected with the CrotchVirus, also known as ACPh6.9. People are self-quarantining although it's not an official mandate as of yet. The stores are running out of food. People are panicking, hoarding and are starting to loot in the streets. At least they are doing so at a safe distance away from other looters. These are crazy times.

Don Langham, retail store associate: Imagine that. We were told our jobs are non-essential to the benefit of the world. They not only closed our shops indefinitely, but we were also laid off. The unemployment office has so many calls they disconnected the number. You can't get through on the website either. Porn sites have more reliable servers! Why have we been paying taxes into a system that doesn't give a shit about us? This just keeps getting worse and worse with no signs of anything getting better.

Terry Reynolds: There's never been a better time in history to not have any kids.

Jay Hoffman, male nurse: They lied to us about how dangerous this is, so we all walked out. The hospital tried to call our bluff and offered us each gift cards to stay. Not raises. Not additional vacation time when this is over. A fucking gift card! And the CEO was on the news praising how hard we are all working and the hospital gave him a raise. This is typical corporate American bullshit. Well fuck them! Expect the death toll to climb to unbelievable heights now. I'll bet those social media experts will shut their damned mouths now!

Jolene Edwards, food blogger & social media influencer: I have resorted to filling out online quizzes and sharing stupid shit like the 29th photo on my phone or posting my favorite obscure movies without giving anyone an explanation. Is this what common people do on a regular basis while I'm getting paid like a boss? I'd like to start an online questionnaire where I ask people to fill out their credit card information, because let's face it – that's all I'm really interested in.

Devin Silver, novelist: I love lockdown.   I am getting so much done. I've learned I no longer have the darkest thoughts out of everyone I know. I feel a great sense of community since we are all going through this together. Every time I have a great idea for a story line, it seems our lives go in a different direction and I have to revise my outline. This is going to take forever.

Al Lee, spiritual guru: I hope when this is over, people start to appreciate what they had, what they have now and that humanity turns a corner and starts being nicer to each other. We can do this!

Art Myers: How come news crews are not following lock down procedures? They keep showing footage of all the empty beaches and streets. Why aren't they non-essential workers? If it wasn't for all the misinformation they've been spreading all these years, perhaps we would not be in this mess? Are people ever going to wake up from the deep sleep they've been in?

Larry Goodman: As soon as more people can be tested, we are expecting the next few weeks to be very bad. The numbers are going to go up. You know what else will be going up? Deaths, unemployment and most importantly, my ratings! You all love me! The doctors are saying we should lock down for 6-8 months, but I am negotiating a better deal. We can conquer this invisible monster enemy in 4 weeks max. I know what you're thinking – your president is a genius. I'm not going to argue. Let me give you my full assurance, if the time frame I just announced doesn't happen, I will deny I ever said it. In the meanwhile, please put hand sanitizer on everything. Best case, it saves your life. Worst case, you'll smell minty fresh.

Terry Reynolds: At the grocery store, there was a sign that said, "Crackers. One per person." I felt personally attacked.

Chapter 4: Day 30

Dolores Pena, mainstream media: Due to the president's denial of a global epidemic, which led to lots of hospital workers quitting, ACPh6.9 has spiraled out of control into a global pandemic. There are over 1 million people dead and an estimated 10 million people are experiencing burning sensations in their dicks, asses, and pussy holes. Children and pets are dropping like flies. The numbers are rising by the minute.

Jolene Edwards, food blogger & social media influencer: Great. Just great. People are announcing they are taking social media breaks. Well, I'll tell you what — there's nothing else to do so you'll be back. We have all been there before.

Dewey Greer, grocery store chain CEO: We are setting up special early morning hours for senior citizens to shop so they can get their supplies too, as well as a special window for the LGBTQ community. It's the least we can do since they were wrongly discriminated against during the outbreak of the HIV/AIDS crisis.

Terry Reynolds, pandemic comedian: The increase in senior citizen muggings in the early morning hours has increased. That's not a joke. Stop it people!

Cara Wilkerson, hospital chief of staff: It's not confirmed but there is some evidence to support the allegations that pets and children under the age of 13 are helping to spread the disease. We are asking you take these items to special quarantine centers we have set up in each city. You'll receive a claim ticket. If your children and/or pets survive, you can retrieve them once this is over. If you don't comply, we are going to call out the national guard to go door to door. If we have to do that, you'll be massively fined. Please comply.

Ricky Harris, father of four: I cannot believe they are telling us to turn in our children and pets, like they are cattle. I understand they are spreading the virus more rapidly than older people, but this is just heart breaking. On behalf of all the parents out there, I am sorry for this. We need to fight back. I just don't know how to.

Art Myers, conspiracy theorist: They can't do this! This is like genocide. Why are they trying to get everyone's children and pets? To euthanize them, so when this is all over, there is population control? I have never wished to be wrong about anything so much as I hope I am wrong about this. This is not a pandemic, this is a scamdemic!

Terry Reynolds: Self Quarantine Diary, Day 32: Did you know there are 2,772 Cheerios in a box? I counted.

Jeff Richards, liberal news media: We need President Goodman out of here. If for no other reason than not having to hear all my friends bitch about him anymore. I am so sick and tired of it. His misinformation and mismanagement is killing us. This has spread out of control because he refused to admit there was a problem. In the meanwhile, we need to get our pets and children back. The president has blood on his hands. He needs to be held liable for this! I have a sinking feeling that somehow, he'll get off scot free.

Shane Gross, conservative news media: As the president has said many times before, we should all remain calm. Most importantly, rather than taking safety precautions, we should continue to place blame on liberals. We may sound like a broken record, but it's our job to tell the people the news as we see it. There is no proof President Goodman dropped the ball on this. This smells like another failed smear campaign to me. Here the liberals go again with another sad attempt to try and impeach the president.

Jeff Richards: We have multiple angle videos that are dated showing President Goodman denied it until it spread out of control.

Shane Gross: Videos can be manipulated in a post-production studio.

Jeff Richards: You and the public can be manipulated even easier.

Shane Gross: Is this really the time to name call, you pathetic asswipe? We need to fight this invisible monster enemy.

Jeff Richards: There are many enemies at this time. One – the actual virus. Two – the president and all his henchmen. Three – all the people like you who want to waste time placing blame instead of focusing on the real problems.

Kacey Davenport, state governor: To combat this invisible monster virus, we have created a few rules for your safety. We need you to turn in your pets and children. Also, unless it's absolutely necessary, we ask that you stay home. Please do not go for rides in your cars and if you have a backyard, please do not use it. Effective immediately, all non-essential stores are closed. Please do not visit your friends or family. Limit your time talking to them on the phone. Please use government approved video chat calls

on unsecure servers. What you think is private is public.
Restaurants will offer curbside take out only. There will be
no more inside restaurant dining. The white zone is for
loading and unloading only. Weddings, cruises and all
public events are canceled. Parking tickets, taxes and
student loans are still being enforced. We are asking you
cover your entire body including your head when you're
alone in your house. We are aware body suits are
impossible to find. You may have to get creative. You'll
certainly have the time. These rules may change at any
time without notice. Please stay on our website and keep
hitting the refresh button. I'd also like you to join me in
giving a shout out to my mom. Hi mom!

Willard Schultz, celebrity: This is sickening. Half of the fun
of eating is to be seen at a trendy restaurant. If our name
is not constantly out there in the press, do we really exist?
So far, I've had to mop my own floors, cook my own food
and do my own laundry. Why, you ask?   Because my
assistant chose to self-quarantine with her family instead
of me. Well, she's fired. I can't wait to block her claim

when she files for unemployment. Who's going to do my hair, my toes and drain my pool? I haven't felt this unhappy since I had my original nose.

Terry Reynolds: How many people learned today their careers are considered useless by the masses?

Dolores Pena: Pet stores and day care centers are being turned into make-shift quarantine centers. They are being guarded by the military.   Record numbers of pets and children are dead. Seems they are dying quicker than anyone else. No one knows why. The death toll continues to rise exponentially, and we are not seeing any light at the end of the tunnel.

Ann Mathis, victim of spousal abuse: I wish I could turn my husband in and keep our children. Without my kids as a buffer, I am afraid my husband is going to turn me into a human punching bag. I went to my pharmacist the other day and I was frantically trying to give him a safe word to let him know my life was in danger. He told me I should drink a glass of water.

Virgil Moss, psychic: Funny that people used to talk shit on astrology in favor of trusting the news media. Maybe this is not the big brother that literature prophesized, but it's certainly like permanent Mercury in retrograde.

May Nash, condo owner: Everyone in my apartment building died. I was trying not to loot, but curiosity got the better of me. I learned my neighbors were hoarders. It's good my next-door neighbor died. Turns out she had a ton of matchbooks and kept them right by the stove. It's lucky she didn't burn the place down. My neighbors in 6A, well, they were annoying. I pretended to like them, but I'm not sad they are gone. The truth is, if I hadn't lived in such close proximity to them, I probably wouldn't have hung out with them at all. Don't get me started about the doorman. Biggest blabber mouth I've ever met. I'd tell him stuff about my life not realizing he was going to tell every single person what I told him in confidence. I gotta get out of here. This place is like a morgue. Literally.

Shawn Cordova, business executive: People ask me how I am surviving. I don't know to be honest. I hate the way hand sanitizer makes me feel, so I don't use it. I prefer organic soap. I'm certainly not wearing a body suit at all times like President Goodman tells us to do. Besides, I've had a pretty good ride. After my boyfriend died, his phone was confiscated and there are pictures of my dick on it. This is the perfect time to die. Especially if things keep up on this path.

May Nash: It's our social responsibility to not be selfish and comply with the rules. But we've got people watching the news all day who don't comprehend a thing mixed with the selfishness of humans. It would be nice if it only affected them and their genitals, but this can touch all of us. It's not fair. Hopefully you lived before this, because the future is contaminated. So many lazy fucks would never leave the house before this crisis and now that they can't, suddenly everyone wants to go out! It's bad enough to have to fight the virus, but we also have to combat stupidity. Ahhhh!

Virgil Moss: If people don't heed the warnings, we are going to have martial law. If you think things suck when we have to self-quarantine on the honor system, just wait until there are armed guards on every street. I hate using the phrase, but we are gonna arrive at a new normal. I assure you, it's going to be filled with even more restrictions than there are now.   Some say the end is near, but I see it differently. I think the beginning is near.

Art Myers: Things are never going to go back to the way they were. Remember 9/11? While we were all freaking out about an invisible enemy called terrorism, they swooped in and started imposing laws to take away our rights. Sound familiar? People didn't do their homework because it sounds ludicrous that we were lied to. We all saw the video footage.   But did we examine all the impossibilities in it? This is where we failed as a society and we should never forget it!

Debra Curtis, grocery store clerk: How come we are on the front lines making little more than minimum wage? We are exposed to all these sick people and they are not doing anything to protect us. We are not doctors saving lives, but we are providing people with food. If you think we want to sweat our asses off in doomsday suits and work 14-hour shifts, you're dead wrong! After all the hospital workers quit, the number of sick people grew exponentially, so if they don't start protecting us and treating us better, we are all outta here. Then everyone is going to be fucked!

Dewey Greer, grocery store CEO: We've offered everyone a pay increase of $1, but unfortunately, by the time taxes are taken out, it doesn't equate to anything, and it puts people in higher tax brackets. If we keep having to raise our worker's rates, our profit margins are going to be much lower. If it happens, we will have to close our stores. The choice becomes, which is more important to the public: fair pay or eating each night?

Devin Silver, novelist: I've been trying to talk to people about what they are going through, but they are dying before our scheduled chat. This is terrible. What I do know is people are in tremendous amounts of pain in their genital region. Doctors and grocery store workers are dying. Somehow politicians are staying alive. It's not fair! This is not any material I can use in the book.

Terry Reynolds: It's "martial law" not "marshal law" is the new it's "you're" not "your."

Larry Goodman, President of the United States: It's been proven by sources hand sanitizer will help protect you from spreading the virus. Please use it, and I don't like saying this word, but I will – liberally. Don't be conservative with it. But try not to buy it from liberal corporations. There are plenty of government approved companies. We'll be providing a list.

Virgil Moss: I see evil coming from the top. They are spreading lies and misinformation to the weak-minded people that are never going to investigate further. People are going to fight with each other when the truth comes out because they will not understand it. What I don't see is why they are doing this. They have something more sinister in mind.

Patti Perkins, airline CEO: We are imposing a travel ban until further notice. Until we get a handle on ACPh6.9, it's imperative people self-quarantine. Do not treat this as a snow day or a free day from work. That means, do not get together with your friends. That means, do not go on dates. Do not go to public places and spread germs. And for God's sake, stop having orgies!

Barbara Higgins, entrepreneur: We are selling shirts with the hashtag "StayInYourFuckingHome" and "Don'tbeselfish." The shirts will retail for $28 each. 50 cents from each sale will be donated to help the people. Apologies in advance for the mail workers that are going to have to risk their lives to deliver these shirts so people can share them on their social media channels.

Sarah Cole, small business owner: Why aren't rich people helping? What about the churches who don't pay taxes anyway? Where are the celebrities opening their wallets? Do certain actors and actresses need their 7 homes when there is a travel ban? This is unacceptable. I hope this sparks a movement for people to wake up and realize these people are not our friends. We supported them, paid for their mansions and now there is a global crisis, they've turned their backs on us. We should turn our backs on them!

Jimmy Rios, mainstream media: People are starting to burn down churches. They are claiming they've prayed all these years and now that they need some relief from a higher power, there is none. Fire fighters and police are being stretched thin as these mini riots are happening all over the globe.

Zack Finley, firefighter: Please folks. Do not take this out on religion. If you do, please do it from your own homes. Burning down buildings is not only dangerous for the community at large, but every time you leave your house, you are potentially spreading infection. If you must leave your house to start fires, please wear protective gear and stand 10 feet apart from your fellow arsonists so you don't potentially infect others.

Terry Reynolds: It's harder to score rice and pasta than it is to get cocaine. The good news is my drug dealer said he will start carrying it.

Frankie Palmer, police chief: Folks. Rioting and looting is not going to help anything at this time. The world is having a global crisis right now so can you please stop being so selfish? We realize celebrities are not donating money or resources, but this is not the time for a witch hunt. There is plenty of time to get even with them.

Tim Francis, priest: Please stop burning down the churches. God will provide for you. He always does. It might not seem that way now. It might seem He has not heard your prayers. It might seem grim, but please trust that He will eventually save us. Send us your money and we will make sure that it goes to rebuild our churches so that when this is all over, you have a nicer place to worship the Lord.

Terry Reynolds: 5,676,321 bottles of beer on the wall, 5,676,321 bottles of beer. Take one down, pass it around, wipe it all off to make sure there are no germs on it, 5,676,320 bottles of beer on the wall... Sing along!

Dean Alonzo, Environmentalist: Interestingly enough, with less people, cars and airplanes out there, the environment is getting cleaner. Imagine that. Maybe it's people that are the virus. In other news, the weather is going to be absolutely perfect for the next few days. Pity no one is allowed to go out.

Nick Hopkins, stock market investor: I've lost everything. The economy is about to completely collapse. There are going to be more riots in the streets. The haves are becoming the have nots and they know what they will be missing out on. You guys better prepare.

Mary Keaton, hand sanitizer CEO: We have people working round the clock to make sure we don't run out of hand sanitizer, thanks to this new government contract. It's very strange they asked us to change some of the ingredients, but this is a very important deal for us, so we are happy to comply. Our magic hand sanitizer elves will not rest until the whole world has enough.

Marcus Donald, college student: School is canceled for the rest of the semester. We get to home school. Positives – I can learn while naked. Negatives – I have a hard time staying focused because I am naked.

Marla Chado, mother of two: I've been homeschooling my children since this pandemic started. The kids are a nightmare! I caught one of them trying to cut class. One of them was trying to throw the teacher out the window.

Also, the teacher was drinking and smoking weed on the job. Yeah, I know. I'm the teacher!

Don Langham, retail store associate: We've all been fired. The stores are closed permanently. We don't know if they'll ever reopen. To be honest, I was living paycheck to paycheck. I think I am going to be homeless. My landlord offered to defer my rent but once this is all over, I have to pay it back all in one payment. Where am I supposed to get the money? The only jobs available are working at grocery stores. It was one thing when I was making crap money with no risk, but I'm not about to put my life in danger for barely above minimum wage.

Shawn Cordova, business executive: I don't know why some people are getting sick and dying yet others are showing no symptoms at all. I wish we had some answers so we could know what to do and how to move forward.

Kacey Davenport: I totally get it. It sucks giving up your children and your pets. But it's too dangerous for the rest of us. We all need to submit and make sacrifices for the greater good. The less selfish you are now, the less the rest of us will have to suffer. It's simple. If you're not going to comply, we're going to start calling the police on you. I am not going to risk my life because you had to have a little fucking brat running around.

Art Myers: The hand sanitizer. Don't use it. That's what's making this get worse. President Goodman is in on it. Go back and look at footage of the older press conferences. He said it repeatedly we should all use as much hand sanitizer as we can. Reporters need to call him out on this and make him explain himself. What they will probably do instead is let him change the subject and sweep this issue right under the carpet in full view of the world!

Jolene Edwards: I have been posting live videos of myself and no one is watching. I guess I am not as popular as I once was. Someone mentioned to me I am tone deaf for posting videos inside my multi-million-dollar kitchen while a lot of people are about to be homeless. I don't see it that way at all. Sending a message of hope to my legions of fans while wearing expensive outfits is inspiring people to be all you can be once this ends.

Pearl Conway, celebrity: They are saying we need to stay in and isolated so we can flatten the curve. But I spent over three hundred thousand dollars on plastic surgery. Curves have always been in and they better make a comeback. If they don't, I am going to sue my doctors. I am so outraged right now, I can't even! I hate this social distancing thing because if you take a selfie with more than one other person in it, it's illegal and punishable by law.

David Trebor, recovered from ACPh6.9: The good news is I can touch my cock again without wanting to kill myself. I cannot masturbate and it still burns a lot when I wake up with a hard on, but I feel so much better than I did about 10 days ago. Good news people, this is no longer a death sentence.

Liam Waters, college student: People are recovering. It's not killing everyone. Why do we have to take this seriously? It's hot outside and I want to go to the beach. I finally don't have exams to study for and I don't have to work because my job is apparently non-essential, whatever that means. I want to go to the beach to party. The only thing good about this is I can now go back to spelling "laugh out loud" instead of "LOL" in texts since I have so much free time.

Andy Massey, artist: It's hard to stay creative. Well, the world is going to have to earn back my gift. I've given and given. They are just trying to take me down. Fuck that! I went out to the store to get more art supplies and I got shamed for not having a face covering. Not wearing a mask in public is the new unprotected sex.

Marsha Stewart, parent: We have 3 kids and a dog. I dropped them off this morning at a center. It was one of the hardest things I've ever had to do. I cried and cried. I have to say, now I've had a chance to see how life is without them, it's kind of awesome. I've gotten to sleep in. No walking the dog in cold weather. No more picking up shit, from either the dog, or the kids. It'll be nice to get them back when this is all over, but I kind of feel like I'm on vacation! Gotta take the good with the bad like my father always used to say.

Sarah Cole: Fucking vandals burned down my store! We had boarded it up and everything, but we didn't even think about our one fatal flaw. The wood we used is not flame retardant. In fact, the fire crew said because the windows were boarded up, it went even faster.

Brian Garcia, lead singer of The Hands: I did a "concert from my kitchen" and I hardly got any viewers. I guess no one wants to hear acoustic versions of my songs. Maybe studio wizardry is what made our music so popular? I have a good body, so I am not above performing shirtless. These are crazy times, so we do what we have to do to get by.

Mary Brooks, millionaire: What are we supposed to do during this time? Read books? There's nothing good on TV, I've binge watched everything and all the productions are shut down. Everything is closed. All I do now is go to the fridge and eat. I am going to become as big as a house! I miss my personal trainer. I can't see my friends. I feel so common. Is this what it's like for poor people? This kind of life is not for me.

Warren Drake, disaster response team: People. Stay home. Home. H. O. M. E. Do not go out. Do not hang with your friends. Do not expose yourself to other people. Stay home. Anyone not following this simple request is part of the problem. We have hidden cameras set up all over. We will be posting your photo on the internet along with your name and address. We will track you through your phones, we will bug your homes, lock you up in jail or whatever it takes to keep you safe. This is not a joke. This is not a drill. We are not messing around. Social distancing is a stupid term that sounds like it was concocted in the same lab as ACPh6.9. I mean, it sounds made up. But we need you to follow it. PLEASE!

Chloe Goodman, stock market investor: Nothing is worth anything. Might as well wipe my ass with my stock certificates. I might have to. In addition to everything else, there's a toilet paper shortage. When this is all said and done, I owe my broker a fee.

Willy Watson, self-isolating: If this virus doesn't kill my wife, I am going to. How come I never noticed how annoying she is? She never stops talking. She never stops complaining. She acts like this is a personal attack on her. She says the protective gear gives her a rash so she can't wear it. We are all going through the same stuff. I can't take it anymore! Every day, I ask her how she's feeling and she thinks I am being loving and attentive. When she says she feels fine, my heart sinks.

Todd Campbell, suffering from ACPh6.9: They don't allow us to see our family or friends. We are going to die here alone. They stuck me in a room with a broken TV that barely gets any reception. The only channel I get is the religious channel. I have the bible memorized by now, but I don't believe in any of this stuff. I've been praying to die for weeks and no such luck. There is no God!

Serena Rowlands, child in quarantine: All of my friends are dead. School is canceled indefinitely. My parents are freaking out because they can't see me. They are allowed to call me, but I sometimes let it go to voice mail just to make them panic. I just want to go outside and play. They won't let me because we are quarantined. My birthday is next week. My party was canceled for obvious reasons. Everyone is telling me to cheer up and be optimistic. Fuck them all hard and deep!

Jeremy Chung, teacher: As soon as this is all over, any students that are still alive are going to wish for death because they are going to have so much homework, they won't even know what hit them. Plus Saturday school. No particular reason for that other than I just want to be a dick.

Larry Goodman: Hope everyone is doing well. I don't know about you, but I'm great! I know we've all been flooded with bad news recently. I have one more thing to add. Once this is over, I am going to have to raise taxes to try to stimulate the economy.   The market is not looking so good right now. Yes, analysts have been saying it goes down every time I give a press conference, but what do they know?   Most of them are high on pills making decisions that affect your livelihood! I've been there too.

Dolores Pena: The death toll is going up.   We've lost famous people from all walks of life including singers, politicians, actors, heads of companies, ministers, news broadcasters and of course a shit ton of common folks like teachers, grocery store workers, doctors, lawyers and cops. There is chaos in the streets.

Esteban Villanueva, mortician: We've officially given up on trying to bury everyone. There are too many of them. Just step over bodies when you pass them in the streets. Don't risk touching them. A dead body can still pass on the germs. Please stop calling us asking about your dead loved ones. There's nothing more we can do.

Art Myers: So many evil people are dying. It's because they trusted their leader. This is what people get when they put profits before human lives. People have attacked conspiracy theorists such as myself for many years and I just have one thing to say: I am alive and you are not. Death is the great neutralizer.

Henry Hughes, former priest: God damn that president. I listened to him and now I am in tremendous pain to the likes of which I've never known before. I never thought I would swear, but I promise you, if this ever gets to you, you'll know where I am coming from. I have prayed and there has been no relief. I renounce God. I ask you to do the same. Fuck this life and fuck that motherfucker! I'm not worried about going to hell sometime in the future. This is hell. Here and now. My balls are the size of a grapefruit.

Terry Reynolds: It's a little-known fact sharks have been on the planet longer than trees.

Shawn Cordova: I woke up in the middle of the night and my balls had swelled up.   I haven't seen anyone, and my dead boyfriend was quarantined weeks ago. It makes me wonder if the information that came from the government was incorrect. If so, was it intentional? I don't trust them at all, so I don't know.

Larry Goodman: There is no need to worry. I am one of the richest people in the country. I can afford the best doctors and care around, so no matter what, I have access to the best treatment, so don't you fret over me. I will continue to be your leader.

Art Myers: He's going to try to become leader of the world. We've been hearing about a new world order for a long time. Everyone dismissed it as a rumor, but I think the time is upon us. The coming days, weeks and months are going to be crucial.   Remember – social distance, don't touch your cock, and trust no one! Not even me!

Dolores Pena: As the death toll continues to rise, people are starting to question the words of President Goodman. The disapproval is making him act like a petulant child instead of a leader. His approval rating is going down at a rate only rivaled by that of the stock market.

Terry Reynolds: What are robbers supposed to do? They can't work because everyone's at home.

Craig Franco, social media enthusiast: Every time a new article comes out, I repost it immediately. Even though I didn't write it or check for accuracy, I love the attention I get when I share it with my followers. I don't have time to look up the credits for a picture I am posting or for a joke I'm stealing. My followers are stupid and they think I am insanely talented. Why should I ruin their day with the truth? I love attacking anyone whose opinion is different from mine. I know I am right and I will convince them. It makes me feel so connected in the global conversation. Also, that conspiracy theorist Art Meyers is so dumb. The things he says sound plausible, but he's been wrong about almost everything he says, or at least some of it.

Terry Reynolds: During this time, if you're bored, you're boring.

Chapter 5: Day 120

Dolores Pena, mainstream media: Millions more are dead tonight after following additional incorrect advice from the president without fact checking.   President Goodman mentioned that wearing a plastic bag tightly over your face for 10 minutes could be used to protect yourself from ACPh6.9. The information was technically correct, but the protection he mentioned resulted in suffocation by death. He has since denied saying it.

Art Myers, conspiracy theorist: Some call it a tragedy. I call it Darwinism.   Survival of the not totally stupid and weak-minded. I've been saying this all along. Why is this so hard to understand? Listen to his advice and you're going to get killed. He does not care about you! It's not just him. He's part of a larger system that wants to keep people down. Hopefully this tragedy is the wakeup call people need. If not, we'll keep repeating this exercise until people learn. Each time the stakes get higher.

Terry Reynolds, pandemic comedian: Remember the person who wanted to argue politics with you? They called you names because you didn't support the president. Well that person is dead.

Esteban Villanueva, mortician: I repeat. Please do not call us about your loved ones. There are too many bodies. Just wrap them in plastic to get them out of the way. That's all we can do at this time. The waiting list for burials is 8 years long and that's if we could do 10 to 12 a day, 7 days a week. It's just not possible.

Dolores Pena: Following the president's advice is the new "Don't drink the Kool-Aid."   People are protesting from home.   There's been a global video chat set up, but it's crashing servers and it's not secure. Also, participants are not muting their lines and it's driving everyone insane. People are being advised to complain via social media only at this time.   Heaven knows, there are enough experts on there to think their words are making a difference.

Jessie Sanders, restaurant worker: Please try to conserve your stash. We are starting to run out of food. We no longer have a menu of items you can choose from. We are just using whatever we have left. If you are one of the chosen ones who gets through to order a meal, you'll have to take what we sell you. Sorry in advance if you are a finicky eater, but there is no other option at this time.

Virgil Moss, psychic: The tide is starting to turn. The president is in danger. Selfishness and inhumanity towards others is falling out of favor and caring for the world as a whole is making a comeback very slowly. Beware President Goodman. If you don't change your ways, you're going to wind up dead. Someone close to you wants your power.

Larry Goodman: The hospitals are out of beds, so unfortunately, some non-vital citizens are going to have to give up their lives for the vital ones. Sorry old people. You've lived. You've experienced. This is a small sacrifice you can make for the greater good. Sorry to all the children who will not get the chance to live great and exciting lives like mine. This was not the scenario we cooked up, but this is our reality, so we all just have to get on with it. We are going to open commerce up again because otherwise, the entire economy is going to collapse. I will remind you of my campaign slogan which was "choose profits over people." This is what got me elected. Don't forget it.

Cara Wilkerson, hospital chief of staff: We've had a dramatic turn of events. The curve has flattened from people dying of ACPh6.9. Now people are starting to die because they are taking the advice of President Goodman. People! Do not be stupid. He is not a qualified medical professional. When are you all going to learn that all he cares about is money? He keeps saying it and you keep not listening.

Art Myers: They are also not mentioning people are committing suicide in large numbers. There's violence in the streets and people are dying from that. They are taking all these statistics and blaming it on ACPh6.9. They are doing this to keep you scared and to keep people locked down. Wake up world!

Henry Hughes, former priest: We need a new religion. Jesus does not represent us. We had 2000 years to listen to his words and we did not. We failed. We need a new solution. The words of the Buddha are just words. If the wisdom was so great, why didn't people heed that advice? Look where we are at. People are dying off in record numbers. Nobody can agree on anything. Humanity is the virus. Can't you see? We need to change the way we all think and act. Globally.

Art Myers: Things are never going to go back to the way they used to be. The more we start accepting that and try to write a new play book which takes everyone into account, the quicker we will get through all this.

Mark Parker, celebrity: I know ordinary people supported me and that's why I live in a mansion. I relate to the people. We are all equal and I love all my fans, but I am asking them to please don't show up at my 15-bedroom home. I have security guards risking their lives to keep me away from all you sickies. The best way for me to get closer to you is to sell autographed photos on my website for hundreds of dollars apiece. Quantities are limited so I advise you to purchase as soon as you can. I can't think of a better way to stay connected than this. Remember, we are all one.

Jolene Edwards, food blogger & social media influencer: Later today, I'll be broadcasting live from my shower. I don't have any symptoms, so for money, I'll be sticking things in my cooch. I hope you'll watch and tell all your friends. I never thought it would get to this, but I am about to lose my mansion. If this happens, I am going to be common. I have way too much pride for that to happen.

Brian Garcia, lead singer of The Hands: I've tried performing covers and acoustic versions of our songs. Nothing is working. I'm going to post my first jack off video later. I have no other options. I'm out of money and I have a lot of creditors.

Larry Goodman: Doctors have been contradicting me in the media and it hurt my feelings, so I've changed my strategy. I've been working with the best philanthropists in the world. Ozzie Madden is a fine person and a great friend of mine. He thinks he might have a vaccine for this dreadful CrotchVirus. We're doing testing on some people that are on death's door. If they die, they were already one foot in the grave so it's no big loss. We're going to be rolling out these tests as soon as possible, so hold your bloomers.

Art Myers: Where's the revolution? How long are we going to let this go on? Every day that maniac is in office is another day we put our lives at risk. He's peddling a vaccine and will order us all to take it. It's going to make everyone sick and kill us all. It will probably have some sort of microchip that will track our every move which will eventually be used to control us and restrict whatever tiny little freedoms we have left. The writing is on the wall.

Debra Curtis, grocery store clerk: We've been busting our asses and risking our lives for what? Measly pay that is now worthless? Well guess what. This is going to come to an end. When it does, all of you fuckers are going to starve to death. I hope you're all happy for listening to that maniac in charge. Whatever happened to thinking for yourselves?

Al Lee, spiritual guru: The time is upon us for a spiritual revolution. This crisis has made us realize all we really need is love. Everything else is not necessary. We burned through resources instead of replenishing them. We used people instead of nurturing them. We lied to people instead of telling them the truth. This is a golden opportunity to reset the evil ways of human nature and live in Utopia. There's plenty for everyone. If you can't see that, open your eyes and use them! The question you must ask yourself is, why did it take tragedy for people to realize this? Let's fight this battle with love and compassion. This is your stay at home spiritual retreat. Don't just stay inside. Look inside. Don't like what you see? Make changes. A better world can be ours!

Larry Goodman: Utopia does not exist nor will it ever. There's too much financial obligation to take care of. We've seen how you all hoarded toilet paper. We watched as the liberals made everything worse.   We saw how celebrities didn't lend a hand for support.   We saw how badly everyone treated each other before all this mess started. And we see how much you argue with each other after I speak in public. People wonder why the government hasn't told the general population about the existence of aliens. It's simple. We cannot trust the public to have nice things.   Humans will treat each other the same way after this is over. Unless human nature is wiped out completely, there will be no Utopia!

David Trebor, recovered from ACPh6.9: I was on death's door and now I am back. I've had an awakening. We need to make some major changes. The earth is dying. We can make a difference. We have to do better. Not just for me. For all of us. We can do this. People. Please. Let's come together. Not actually coming together. Can't risk getting the CrotchVirus. You know what I mean. Leaders stand up and show yourselves. There's got to be some of you out there.

Amy Mitchell, stockbroker: I think I am going to turn over a new leaf. I spent my whole life trying for money and power. I admit. It tasted good. But now none of it is worth anything. I have regrets. I don't want to spend the rest of my life clutching for worthless paper. I have the chance to give my life some meaning.

Al Lee: Let's learn from our mistakes. This is the reset button we need. We must use this time to write new rules that will apply to everyone.   For all this time, we've only thought about the rich and powerful and all of us had to get in line with that. They don't exist anymore. This is the time to unite.

Dolores Pena: After working from home, people are starting to realize teachers and politicians are not necessary, and famous people are worthless. Most meetings could have been emails. Lots of people have no real purpose in their life other than treating each other awfully in the pursuit of money. After the collapse of the stock market, the playing field has finally been leveled. The fact that it took centuries for people to realize how selfish we all are has made everyone full of regret.

Chris Ravinna, medical patient: I was in a coma for months. I opened my eyes and the doctor told me what is going on in the world. I've been asleep in a peaceful state. Now I'm awake and people are dying in record numbers. The streets are on fire. There is chaos everywhere. What is happening? Put me back to sleep! I don't want to go out into this world. I will probably die anyway because my immune system has been compromised so severely.

Jeremy Chung, teacher: Imagine how it feels to learn the thing I've dedicated my life to is now considered useless by the public at large. I am hurt, in shock and a little bit bitter to tell you the truth. On top of that, we have to be paranoid about who and what we can trust. There is so much conflicting information out there, I've become a hypochondriac. It all sounds true and it all sounds preposterous at the same time. Everyone I talk to says the same thing. At least we can agree on that! I can't take this anymore.

Al Lee: Karma has no expiration date.

Mary Nash, condo owner: So like all of my family and friends are dead. All of them. Every single one. In less than 6 months, I've lost every person I know one by one. The grief has been insurmountable, but it's nothing compared to the smell of dead bodies everywhere. I have no one to talk to. No one to confide in. The news asked me to tell my story and now strangers won't get anywhere near me because they think I'm contagious.

Marcus Donald, college student: My teacher is dead, so I am glad I decided to procrastinate in doing my assignments. The only bad thing is, that guy owes me $10 and I let him borrow my watch. I know currency is worthless, but it's the principle. I was studying to be a teacher and that career is dead on arrival. Is the college going to give my parents their money back? I doubt it.

Brian Garcia: I'm not gay, but I would be willing to suck dick on camera. I am hungry. I am scared. Most of the band is dead. My life is pretty much over at this point. I don't know what else to do. Please send help. I haven't eaten in days.

Terry Reynolds: The only way to find out if you're truly sick is to rub your genitals on a celebrity and wait for their test results.

Jessie Sanders, restaurant worker: We are running out of food. This is the end. What are we going to do? Our suppliers have nothing. There's more demand than product. Truck drivers are dead. Farmers are dead. Our cooks are dead. Factory workers are dead. Try to grow your own food if you can. If you can't, it's over. This is it. We're starving too. To all the people that hoarded, I hope you're happy. I take that back. I hope you are the ones who suffer the most and die miserable deaths.

Terry Reynolds: Where are the zombies? I've seen every end of the world movie there is. I feel cheated.

Dick Davison, doorman: 95% of the residents in the building are dead. I just sit at the front desk all day. No deliveries. No packages. There's literally nothing to do. I thought this job was boring before, but now, it's even worse. Also, it's so dangerous because everyone that comes and goes has to pass by me first. There are no jobs to be had right now, so I am stuck here.

Ben Branch, baseball player: Grateful I have a huge house with a home gym so I can exercise, but I haven't been able to play catch because everyone is dead. I did a video call with some of my teammates to throw the ball around for practice and now all my windows are broken.

Art Myers: People are going to turn their backs on celebrities. The remaining public has had enough of the braggarts. The reason so many celebrities have survived this crisis is because they are behind the protective walls of their mansions. Get ready famous folks. The general population is coming for you.

Phoebe Little, celebrity: Oh no. The armed guards outside my mansion have died. I discovered it this morning when I was trying to radio them on the walkie talky. I called out. When they stopped replying, I thought they were playing a prank. I threatened to cut their salary if they didn't answer me. There was just silence. My 2nd assistant confirmed the bad news. What am I going to do? I heard people are mad at celebrities. I'm worried.

Gregory Stephen, father of two: Just because you had one hit pop song many years ago, I really don't care to hear your thoughts on what's happening in the world. Times are different now. And now that we've all seen the insides of your mansions, I have to ask – who are your decorators? You people have awful taste and lots of you are hoarders.

Neil Wong, mainstream media: It's too dangerous to go outside. If you can avoid leaving your house all together, we would recommend it. Not only is there a great chance you could catch ACPh6.9, but all across the world, people are starting to riot. They are obeying the social distancing ordinance but that means there are people everywhere. The celebrity march is taking place live as we speak. Famous people, you better watch your asses and ass implants!

Larry Goodman: Tentative release date for the vaccine: Christmas of next year. Ho Ho Ho!

Art Myers: This is population control. I advise everyone to stay away. It's unclear how they are going to force this so-called cure on everyone, but I am warning you – I see very bad things coming from this. The effects of the vaccine will be way worse than ACPh6.9. It's going to kill a lot of people and it will control the ones who survive.

Joseph Simpson, hotelier: We haven't had a customer since this began. I wish they would have let us use our facility for a hospital or something. We have people dying alone in the streets and all these gigantic buildings are empty. This was not well thought out at all.

Barbara Higgins, entrepreneur: My company is working on manufacturing a pair of protective underwear that will prevent people from touching their genitals in case there is ever another outbreak. We are playing around with names, but so far "Cock Blocker" is in the lead. If it sells, we will work on "Tit Blocker" next.

Jeremy Chung, teacher: I was supposed to have a video chat with my students. No one showed up. It turns out, they are all dead. Do you know how many funeral campaigns parents are going to want me to donate to?

Frasier Blake, alcoholic: I was ok when strangers started dying. I was ok when people I knew started dying. I was ok when people were hoarding food. Now there's an alcohol shortage. This is the end!

Andy Massey, artist: I've spent all this down time creating art. Most of my clients are dead and I'm running out of room in my studio apartment. I've had to stack the paintings and I'm sleeping on canvas. My back is killing me. I've never thought of art as product, but if I don't get rid of my current stock soon, I am going to be living a hoarder's life.

Frank Simpson, divorcee: My wife asked me for a divorce. That's a laugh. Of all times to decide she hates me. When everything turns to shit. It's practically impossible to get a lawyer. Well, she's getting nothing. If I am lucky, she'll get the virus.

Al Lee: If this ever ends, we should not go back to normal. Normal didn't work. That's why we are here. We gave the government so much of our salary for most of our lives. When we needed to rely on them, what did they give us? The bare minimum. They gave us laws and restrictions we didn't need or want. They refused to provide us all with health care. They hid important information from us. The things they often told us were full of lies and mistruths. So many of these people can't even be punished because they are dead.

Terry Reynolds: I've been avoiding people since long before all this started. Where's my medal of honor? I plan to avoid people long after this is all over.

Virgil Moss: New laws are coming. New ways of life. People are warning of a new normal. It's not really new. It's sure not going to be normal. Human nature is something to beware. If we want to learn anything from this tragedy, we need to change our behavior and almost everything about society as it currently stands.

Shep Farley, building construction: They've halted all of our projects indefinitely, so when people see lots of incomplete buildings all over their cities, this is why. We think it looks like shit. It sends a bad message that makes it look like civilization is on its way out, but if you have a complaint, talk to my boss. That's above my pay grade.

Jack Walters, medical professional: If the country reopens for business and people stop self-quarantining, this is going to get even worse. Medical professionals should be in charge of giving advice at this time, not politicians and philanthropists. For your own safety, please fact check before you decide to be stupid and put all of our lives at risk.

Terry Reynolds: How many people does it take to change a lightbulb? You can't. Everyone is dead.

Paul Connors, environmentalist: It's amazing when you take people out of the equation, the world starts to repair itself. Crime has gone down. Schools are shut down and classroom shootings have stopped. Pollution has gone down. Contamination of our bodies of water have gone down. What's not going down is people being selfish. People need to stop thinking, "This is not going to happen to me." It IS going to happen to you and everyone you meet if you don't stop being so careless and stupid. How many times do we have to tell you this? Also, people aren't going down on each other, but we appreciate those who are following the rules.

Josh Rao, formerly in lockdown: I had quarantined myself all this time, but I got lonely, so I went on a dating app and I met up with someone. I asked him if he'd been self-isolating. He should have said, "No. I was self-loathing." He lied to me and now I have the CrotchVirus. It hurts. I wish I hadn't been so foolish. I hope people listen to my story because I am in more pain than I've ever been in. Use my life as a cautionary tale.

Jimmy Rios, mainstream media: A celebrity who recovered from ACPh6.9 is calling for places such as couture clothing stores, tanning salons and beauty parlors to reopen. This reporter wonders what kind of message it sends to folks about the priorities of the people we worship like royalty. We'll be taking your calls.

Caller 1: This is some serious bullshit. I'm happy she's ok but I've been cooped up at home for all this time and I don't think it's fair for the rich to be out there spreading ACPh6.9. I've been seeing reports of hate groups that are rubbing their genitals all over public places because their attitude is, "I'm going to die, so I don't care about people anymore." This is not ok! Something needs to be done about it.

Caller 2: What happened to all those borders that we were building? We don't need physical borders. We need borders in the form of more regulations and more hoops to jump through to avoid this kind of bullshit from happening. It's cheaper for taxpayers too!

Caller 3: This actress makes shitty movies. Just because she knows how to act against green screen, we are supposed to let her do whatever the hell she wants? It's irresponsible and selfish. As soon as this is over and canceling hideous celebrities comes back in fashion, she's officially canceled! That reminds me. What happened to "woke" culture? Are they all asleep?

Jolene Edwards: I was talking with some other social media influencers and I heard this rumor there was a new technology that was giving us all cancer. They are saying ACPh6.9 is a smoke screen to divert our attention from that. I posted about it on social media and now everyone thinks I'm crazy. Maybe it's false. Who knows? Anything sounds possible to me at this point. After rumors started spreading, the internet police have taken down every article on the subject. What I want to know is that if it's not true, why was it censored? What do they have to hide? I am not promoting violence. I'm promoting myself!

Chapter 6: Day 365

Dolores Pena, mainstream media: Fuck Fuck Fuck Fuck! There's no point in sugar coating anything anymore. If you've been in a coma for the last year, consider yourself lucky. Let's briefly get you up to speed. The government denied the existence of ACPh6.9, also known as the CrotchVirus or the invisible monster enemy. By the time it was acknowledged, it had spread all over the world and killed millions. In lieu of a cure, the government advised using hand and body sanitizer to kill the virus. Unfortunately, the ingredients were tainted and anyone who used it had an allergic reaction which was worse than the CrotchVirus itself. It has been alleged that President Goodman was in cahoots with Mary Keaton, the CEO of the government approved manufacturer of the deadly hand and body sanitizer. She has since died of ACPh6.9. Somehow, this has not affected the president's approval rating at all. In fact, he is more popular than ever. Scientists are studying to figure out if the virus also affects the brain and people's rational decisions. The economy has tanked, there are riots in the streets and dead bodies everywhere. Misinformation is the new normal and most companies have gone out of business. In happier news, our ratings are stronger than ever.

Tim Francis, priest: Since when can they say the f-word on TV? Jesus Christ!

Jack Walters, doctor: There are over 50 million people dead. The numbers are still not going down, some 365 days later. The cure the president promised was a lie. Suicides are up, the unemployment rate is astronomical, and the world will never go back to the way it was just one short year ago. Entire family lineages have been wiped out and now that most children are dead, the future of humanity is uncertain.

Kelly Jameson, police force: The virus has caused mass destruction. Some of the side effects have been deaths from rioting in the streets and mass suicides. There are dead bodies everywhere. The smell of burning flesh is a daily reality. Pretty much everything we ever knew and every way of life that was familiar is gone. It escalated so quickly. We no longer have the resources to protect museums, rich people or landmarks. We ask that you please respect these things and not go crazy. There's only one glimmer of hope for us all – the president has finally taken ill! It seems that someone from inside his inner circle gave him the tainted hand sanitizer he'd been advising citizens to use. Justice has finally been served.

Larry Goodman, President of the United States: I was set up by the news media. They want me to take responsibility for this and that's never going to happen. As you know, I have fallen ill but I will continue to serve, make laws and grace your life with my presence until my last breath, which I know, many of you hope will be soon. I have the best care and I'm not planning on going anywhere, so save your victory parties for another day.

Earl Ross, looter: I've never been able to buy fine art, let alone own something from one of the masters. I went to the Museum of Modern Art in New York today and I picked up a Picasso. I would have had more, but I had to bonk people over the head with paintings and they ripped.

Jerry Ramirez, looter: I live in a mansion now. I always dreamed that one day I would have enough money, but it never happened. I got lucky just by breaking the right window. I discovered a dead rich person inside and I took their house. We never really know how life is going to turn out. It also goes to show that a piece of flimsy glass is all that stands in the way between us and them.

Julia Frankel, robber: Robbing a bank has never been easier. I took a lot of cash just in case, but unfortunately, it's not worth anything. I thought everyone would have the same idea as me, but I was the only one there. I wasn't even wearing a mask!

Mary Brooks, millionaire: I am afraid to go outside. I think if I leave my house, this could be the end for me. We have water, but we are famished. I am not just hungry for rich people things like caviar either. Dog food sounds good at this point. I know no one is going to feel sorry for me. Please help me. I am starving!

Terry Reynolds, pandemic comedian: I miss simple things like only worrying about cancer and gun violence when I leave my house.

Art Myers, conspiracy theorist: People are fucking morons. For years, we've been talking about how 99 percent of the people are controlled by the 1 percent. We've given financial statistics to let folks know what side of the fence they are on. We've had info sessions, video tutorials online and we even hosted live events at places such as Occupy Wall Street in New York City. What did people do about it? Diddly squat. This is how we get into situations like this. That is not a conspiracy. That just shows people would rather complain than do anything about it, so here we are. Maybe folks will start listening from now on?

Richard Barry, doctor: An untainted vaccine should be available soon. In the meanwhile, please continue to stay away from others.   If you're experiencing symptoms, please don't touch your crotch. We are working on this as fast as we can.   As you probably imagine, we have interference from a certain person who shall remain nameless. But it rhymes with Harry Couldman.

Jolene Edwards, food blogger & social media influencer: After the alleged conspiracy theory debacle, I learned to keep my mouth shut. People are obsessed with their beliefs. It is not my life's purpose to wake people up. Now when I post things online, I don't get any reaction at all because most of my following is dead. It's official. I'm irrelevant. This is the worst pandemic ever! I regret not doing something more meaningful with my life.   I am not going to self-quarantine anymore. I am going to try and get this so my life ends.

George Bernstein, firefighter: People – please stop burning bodies too close to wood structures. We don't have the manpower. It's just making everything messier. We realize you want to give your loved ones a proper send off, but please don't. Burn them in the streets. For everyone's safety.

Brian Garcia, lead singer of The Hands: I gave up my music career. I decided to put my life to good use, so I started working at a grocery store. I got to see first-hand how grateful people were to be able to get supplies and each day, I felt great. Then one day, some asshole rubbed his crotch on some shopping carts I touched, and I got the fucking virus. This is the end for me. I hope one day people will remember my music, but I am pretty sure I am going to go out as someone who failed in their original career and died making minimum wage.

Jolene Edwards: A group of people broke into my house. They said they were going to gang rape me. I begged them to let me film it in hopes it might revive my career. But they wouldn't. They all took turns and one of them had the virus. Be careful what you wish for. I am in so much pain now. At least it will be all over soon.

Al Lee, spiritual guru: How can we face the future together without fear? How can we move forward instead of backwards? The time is upon us. If we don't rewrite these old and archaic laws, we are going to keep repeating these stupid mistakes. The rules we've been following simply don't work. A new president is not going to fix it. We must act now. The population is reaching a critical moment in a very dangerous time. What's it going to take to make people wake up? Another catastrophe? Something even worse than this one?

Wallace Hopkins, postage stamp collector: I spent my entire life collecting stamps. I have almost every rare one ever released from the last hundred years. The only way I could afford my collection was to forgo going out to nice dinners, seeing friends and having a life. Now this is just a worthless pile of junk. I can't even use them to mail letters since the Post Office has ceased to exist. If I could advise people to collect experiences instead of things, I wish that!

Jessie Sanders, restaurant worker: Once this is over, do we really think anyone is going to want to come into our restaurant and dine in? There's going to be sick people jizz all over everything. No matter how much we disinfect, people are still going to be leery if they have to sit in close proximity to others. We won't be able to afford to keep the restaurant open if we are forced to make our customers social distance. The extreme wait time will anger people and they'll boycott us.

George Fry, poet: An epic poem needs to be written about this point in history. Each new day is unprecedented. I think a great change is coming. The question is, should it rhyme, or should it be like The Odyssey?

Art Myers: People keep trying to debunk the things I say. Some people are calling for my arrest. Have you got nothing better to do in a pandemic? I just want to remind everyone I am merely expressing my opinion and I have not been promoting violence against anyone. If people think there is any harm in that, maybe they need to reexamine themselves.   We follow an archaic constitution, and everyone is ok with that, but what about the part that mentions freedom of speech? People don't realize how wrong I hope I am about these things. If I am not, we are seriously fucked. There's one rule of thumb we should all follow. If you didn't see it yourself, stop trying to be a reporter. It's easier to lie to people than to convince them they've been lied to. Question everything. If you just trust one side of the story, you are part of the problem, spreading more disease than ACPh6.9 ever could.

Jimmy Rios, mainstream media: Conspiracy theorists are coming up with all kinds of stuff to discredit us. They are saying we are just actors reading scripts. It is not true. We've been trained to adlib too.   Just because our respective media companies are owned by billionaires who are insane and have hidden motives, why would people suggest that we have secret agendas? They say we have one-sided reporting designed to upset the masses, keep them confused and angry so they don't have the energy to think about the real problems in the world?   Let me ask you this – has the media ever lied to you?

Terry Reynolds: Seems like everyone is spreading misinformation, but I assure you, anything I say is correct and funny. Starting now!

Frankie Palmer, police: We asked people nicely to stay home, and it's not been working. So we will be increasing our lockdown measures. Don't view it as punishment. It's for your safety. You might think a bunch of sinister shit is happening while you are in your homes, not allowed to protest in groups. Or maybe the technology you've been using to vent about this is being tracked or might even be causing something worse than ACPh6.9. I cannot confirm or deny it, but they say rumors are always true.   The quarantine is over when we say it's over. The sooner you come to peace with that, the happier you'll be.

Pearl Conway, celebrity: Being locked in a mansion is a prison. There's so much to clean. I've got so many more crevices than normal people. I'm still baffled that my staff would rather be with their families than stay here in my mansion. They all could have come along too for a reasonable rate.

Silas Renderman, studio apartment renter: I have to walk back and forth across my floor about 1700 times in order to get some exercise. I feel dizzy all the time, but I don't want to get fat. All I do these days is get up, go to the fridge, eat and then sit on my ass. I don't even like to drink alcohol, but I started to because it makes me sleepy, which causes me to pass out and miss meals.

Bernie Baines, unemployed: It sucks that the government waits until now to tell me my business is non-essential. I had a local restaurant. I regularly donated to the homeless, delivered food to the blind and helped the disenfranchised. Now, I am no longer allowed to go to my business. I've had to lay off my whole staff and I am told that if I go to the store to try and pack it all up, they will arrest me. I took a risk. Because I wasn't wearing a doomsday suit, I received a ticket for $1000. I told the officer that I thought money was not worth anything anymore. He took out a night stick and beat me to the ground. He told me if I dare talk back to him again, he's going to lock me up.   This is not a democracy anymore. This is a police state.

Terry Price, scientist: We can confirm the false medical information that President Goodman has suggested over the last year has contributed to many unnecessary deaths and even more preventable suicides and violence. If you have any of these items, please throw them out immediately. The beauty of science is that it's true, even if you choose not to believe it.

Richard Berry: People are trying to get prescriptions for lethal doses of heroin or pills that keep your brain so numb, you're little more than a vegetable. We want to help people, but I did not sign up to be an assisted suicide doctor. Our supply of toxic drugs is starting to run low because they are in such high demand.

Debra Curtis, grocery store clerk: We've set up odd and even days for grocery store shopping. If your last initial corresponds to an even number, you shop on that day and vice versa. It's strange with so many less people on earth, the lines are still ridiculously long. We can't keep most things in stock. It leads to lots of fighting and shouting when people have waited in line for hours only to get to the front of the queue and we are out of everything.

Rich Berry, restaurant worker: Giving people bad news comes with the territory. How many times have I had to tell a customer, "Your meal is going to be delayed a few moments," or "I'm sorry, my staff didn't listen to your order. They put an item on your plate you said might kill you, so we have to start over, so you don't die." But now, a person orders something and our stock is so low, they get whatever we serve them. It's the worst when someone orders rice or pasta. Come on. Like we have any of that!

It's not going to happen. If times were normal, we would be shut down for health code violations.

Larry Goodman: Rumors of my death have been greatly exaggerated. I am not going anywhere. I am here to stay. I will be in charge until my last dying breath. In the event of my untimely death, I will make sure our Vice President carries out everything I already began.

Basil McGee, Vice President of the United States: Further to what the president said, I promise to be just as effective a leader as he is. I will be just as snappy in my press conferences. I pledge to be petty when it comes to yelling at reporters who ask difficult questions. I will continue to give the rest of the living world reasons to make memes and laugh at me. Because that's what it's all about ultimately. Laughter. Laughter makes the world go round. Especially in these difficult times.

Terry Reynolds: I think we should all call up our exes and apologize for thinking they were the biggest nightmares that ever existed.

Barbara Higgins, entrepreneur: I once had the opportunity to buy the domain www.socialdistancing.com for $1. Like an idiot, I bought www.pandemichoax.com instead. Can you imagine the clout I could have had? This is what I get for trusting conspiracy theories.

Bruce Nelson, suicide hotline operator: This is the first time in history we are not trying to discourage people from killing themselves. We've got so many callers, we give them our usual spiel about why they should want to live. If they can't check any of those boxes, we ask them to kindly not waste any more of our time as the queue of callers is non-stop.

Terry Reynolds: I would like to debunk a popular conspiracy theory that's been circulating – eating an entire box of cookies after midnight will not make you sleep any better.

Dolores Pena, mainstream media: More restrictions are coming your way. Your phones and computers are being used to track how many times you use them to watch porn. If you exceed a certain number of times, your chances of catching ACPh6.9 increase. Even though it conflicts with medical information that was released last week, it's now changed. Again, there is no evidence proving it either way, but this is what we've been told to inform you. It sounds true enough. When we come back from a commercial break, more bad news! Stay tuned.

Devin Silver, novelist: Big brother is not just watching you anymore. Big brother is your actual brother. And your mother and your father. And your mother and father's brother. It's just as confusing as the news. I really want to write an optimistic story about the world, but everything seems so damned depressing. How am I supposed to uplift and inspire when I am down in the dumps? Maybe that should be the focus of my book? When you fall on your face, you're still moving forward.

Dean Chavez, healer: If we look within, we can break the chains of the slavery we face out on the streets. Everything is negative. People are sicker and sadder than ever. There has got to be a way out of this. We can meditate. We can chant. We can focus on the now. If we do that, we are not focused on all the crap that is going on out there in this barren wasteland. If we change our attention, we can change our attitude. Let's do it together. Breathe in. Breathe out. Om.

Alesha Kincaid, former party girl: The one good thing about this quarantine is I haven't had anything to drink or smoke. No sweets, no drugs, no sex. I've been doing home workouts like crazy. I think my cells have revitalized themselves. It's like how the environment is regenerating from humans not being out on the streets polluting up the place. I think the key take away here is that humans are the real virus. Humans are the real disease.

Dolores Pena: Breaking news! President Goodman is dying. He's set to make a speech later today, presumably to step down and let the Vice President take over. If people could march in the streets to celebrate, I think they would.

Larry Goodman: I am too ill to continue running the country, so Vice President McGee is going to take over. Before I go, there are a few things I want to say. As long as the invisible monster disease continues to be out there, none of us are safe. In closing, some of the things you thought were hoaxes were true. We think ACPh6.9 started when we printed more money because government spending had gotten out of control. The printers ran out of ink, so we imported it from overseas. Seems that it was tainted. Eventually, once there is a cure for ACPh6.9, life will return as we once knew it – but with more restrictions. Good luck!

Basil McGee: I am reading off a teleprompter, so please excuse my woodenness as you hear these words. As former President Goodman has mentioned, I am in charge now. The first thing I am going to do as your ruler is postpone any upcoming elections, for your safety. You might think it's because I want unlimited power. I confirm that I am denying it. As you know, we are still working on a vaccine for ACPh6.9, so until there is one, we are going to ask you to stay inside as we continue to take away your rights. If you want this to change, you must rise up and overthrow us. Umm. Excuse me. Is that really what I am supposed to say? I thought we had discussed that certain parts of this speech were supposed to be kept hidden from the public at large.

Teresa Watson, presidential speech writer: I will probably go to jail or be killed for exposing the truth, but I just couldn't take it anymore. So many of my friends and loved ones have been suffering greatly, so if I have to sacrifice myself for the good of humanity, I am happy to be your martyr. Just know that if anything should happen to me, there is truth in what I wrote.

Dolores Pena: Breaking news again. There was a major blunder in the Vice-President's initial speech taking over the duties of President. He said this whole thing was all about control. Speech writer Teresa Watson was killed when her car exploded under totally non-suspicious circumstances.

Andrea Rodriguez, internet police spokesperson: We are taking down all articles that mention this from the internet. They violate our community standards. The ironic thing is we have no standards, but the truth is, we just don't want this kind of info out there. We have the power, not you! Those are the terms and conditions you agreed to.

Art Myers: If they truly wanted us to get better, how come the first things they tell us on the news aren't recipes for health and wellness? Where there's smoke, there's fire.

Al Lee: For a star to shine bright, it takes darkness.

Chapter 7: Year 2

Basil McGee, President of the United States: For the first time since ACPh6.9 began two years ago, the number of deaths attributed to the virus have finally slowed. People are still dying en masse, but it's mostly from drug overdoses and suicide. As you may have heard, former President Goodman is in a coma. After many months of being a vegetable, he started to show signs of improvement. I pulled the plug for everyone's safety. Sadly, he died this morning.

Jimmy Rios, mainstream media: President McGee's approval rating and people's confidence and trust in him is lower than ever before in history. The suicide rate is nearly one in three now. People are sick and tired of these extremely prohibitive lockdown procedures. Since the launch of ACPh6.9, there have been approximately 200 million deaths worldwide.

Marcus Israel, citizen: Do you ever wonder why they keep repeating everything on the news with little or no new information? Repetition of propaganda helps people believe it. Repetition of propaganda helps people believe it. Repetition of propaganda helps people believe it. If you tell a lie enough times, eventually it becomes true.

Kelly Lancuza, citizen: We've been under lockdown for almost two years to the day since this virus came out. Think of all the lifeless pets and dead children. Grief stricken families and dead bodies everywhere. We are now immune to the smell of it. People don't have real jobs anymore. So many people are just trying to grow food and dispose of the deceased. This is not living! This is hell!

Miles Lawson, dentist: As soon as we went into lockdown, the government told me my business was inessential, therefore I had to shut it down. My patients called me when they had issues, but there was nothing I could do for them. They were begging me for assistance. They had no one to turn to except me. Then I had an aha moment. I got into this business so I could help people, so god damnit, I was going to do just that. Power usually equals corruption, but I decided to break the chain. I set up a makeshift office in my basement and I started seeing patients on the down low. It was a big risk, but everyone was so grateful.

Floyd Rice, patient: I had a major dental emergency, and no one would take me. Eventually, I got hooked up with Dr. Lawson. A prince of a guy. We met in his basement and he fixed me up. He had a book in his makeshift waiting room that looked fascinating, so I picked it up. It was called "Post Celebrity." In it, it imagined a futuristic society where the government poisoned a whole bunch of people. It sounded like what was happening now. I asked him about it, and he said that one of his Facebook friends wrote it. He had some witty status updates, but was always self-promoting, so basically to shut the guy up, Miles bought the book. He hadn't actually read it. Typical! Anyway, it led us to a conversation and the next thing we knew, we went down a rabbit hole.

Miles Lawson: Before this whole mess started, friends and colleagues had been talking about the fact that so many things didn't add up. I guess because our lives were pretty good aside from all the governmental interference, we never really questioned things. Then suddenly we were faced with all this free time after we were told our livelihoods were non-essential for the betterment of our country.

Floyd Rice: I had mentioned to Dr. Lawson that I knew a lot of people who were starting to discuss these same things.   It was easy to tell who thought like I did and who didn't. I would make a non-threatening, yet derogatory comment about not believing what I was hearing on the news and if they looked at me like I had 3 heads, I knew to drop it. If I found they chimed in with their own examples of distrust, I knew we were on the same side. It was when I was with Dr. Lawson that we came up with an idea.

Miles Lawson: We would recruit other people that felt as we did. We would call our resistance The Rabbit Hole. If we were to be caught, no one would know what we were referring to. If each member found 10 other members, our movement would gain traction quickly. What kept people oppressed for so many centuries was them staying ignorant. Since we had nothing but time, we turned off our TVs and read as many books as we could get our hands on that talked about the dark web of deceit that had been spun all over the world long ago. This information is not hard to find if you look for it. We started a password protected, living document where people could add their visions for a new world.

Art Myers, conspiracy theorist: The Rabbit Hole. Very interesting. I found out about it because, duh – I am a conspiracy theorist. I usually hate every radical idea that comes my way because by virtue of distrusting everything and everyone, what could convince me that this movement would or even could succeed? But The Rabbit Hole was filled with others like me. Even better, for the first time in recent memory, I was treated with love and respect. After the first full year of lockdown, we started having conference calls. Soon there were hundreds of thousands of us, so we had to start having various heads in different regions.

Perry Bennett, scientist: We missed out initially on extra members, because it was too dangerous to post our ideas on the internet. So we circulated information from our meetings on secure networks. Tecchies will always be able to overpower the muscle! They made fun of us in school, but we've certainly showed them!

Terry Reynolds, pandemic comedian: I have a friend who is a prostitute. She puts the 'ho' in 'hope.'

Devin Silver, novelist: I write slow. I know this. I could have pumped out something, but I am not a machine. I have to be in love with it. Then and only then will it be ready. I've been planning this since the start of the virus. Everything is in my brain. It's almost ready to hit the page. I think it's going to be brilliant. Just wait.

Virgil Moss, psychic: The tide is shifting. The planets are nearing alignment for a great change. They haven't been in this conjunction in hundreds of years. This is a golden opportunity for positive change. Hopefully people have been using this time for inner reflection instead of sitting around watching TV and letting their braincells atrophy. Guess we will all soon find out together.

Barbara Higgins, entrepreneur: I wish the organization The Rabbit Hole would go public. Their ideas are so radical and great, it reminds me of the dotcom boom. There is so much uncharted territory and potential. Whoever came up with this idea is either going to win so big, they will become a living legend, or it will fail so hard, it's going to be of biblical proportions. I would be willing to take the chance and invest though.

Parker Medina, hippie: People have always made fun of me for having ideals of love and peace. It's never gotten me down. I believe in the power of people. Ultimately, we all just want to be loved. You add all this crap to the mix like money, politics, greed and jealousy and it's easy to see how fast the pool gets muddy. What people fail to realize is we're all in that same pool.

Brian Powell, alien researcher: I've been called a quack because I have spent my life researching life on other planets. People try to discredit me. If you search for me on the internet, there are tons of "take down" articles. They accuse me of antisemitism and homophobia. If people did the research, they would learn I am gay and Jewish. I never let it get me down though. People are addicted to their beliefs. There's nothing you can do to make them think otherwise. What I tell people to ask themselves repeatedly is if there is nothing to hide, why does the government suppress stuff like the truth about the JFK assassination, 9/11 or Area 51? They obviously know more than they tell us because they have classified files on them. I've always found it strange that people think I am the crazy person.

Basil McGee: Just checking in to see how lockdown is going for you? People have been accusing us of a term called "gaslighting." It's defined as the manipulation into doubting your own sanity. I doubt any of these things are true. If you believe them, you're probably insane. Plain and simple.

Miles Lawson: As The Rabbit Hole grew and grew, we acquired people from all industries into our collective. We had doctors, lawyers, former politicians, scientists, artists, philosophers, computer geeks and drug addicts. We welcomed everyone equally. The only criteria was that we were united in our thinking that we had to find a way to topple the evil politicians. We gave everyone a homework assignment in our communities and that is to come up with radical ideas to help us achieve our goal.

Courtney Globo, The Rabbit Hole member: Usually in organizations you've got weak links. People claim they are on your side, but when it comes down to it, they are incompetent, or they say they are going to do one thing, yet they actually do another. In this army, everyone is united for one goal: to get our rights and our livelihoods back. They've taken everything away from us. Now we've got nothing. Leaving your house once a week to get groceries that are owned by the state is no way to live. Our babies are dead. Our pets are dead. What is their end game? We will not let them control us anymore. When this is all over, we will be victorious!

Dolores Pena, mainstream media: As President McGee imposes more restrictions, we are still no closer to a cure. The big topic of debate is when the world finally reopens again, what will life be like? The world has much fewer people and there are no pets or babies. What is the future of humanity? Plus what industries will be killed off for good? Sports players, you'd better watch those cute little butts!

Tim Francis, priest: I keep telling my followers to continue praying. Jesus is going to get us through all this. Don't stop believing. I can feel it that He's going to save us all from this mess.   The more you donate, the closer we get to salvation. It's pretty simple, really.

Jesus Cristos, recovering drug addict and drug dealer: A long time ago, I used to sell drugs. Now I only take them sometimes.   Instead of injecting myself with vaccines, I dosed myself with heroin. While everyone was miserable with ACPh6.9, I was high as fuck. Anyway, when I was a dealer, I covered the Washington DC area. My clients were some of the top politicians. At the time, senator Basil McGee was a big customer. He was a huge junkie. How he managed to keep it a secret is beyond me because he was a mess! Lots of people have bad things to say about him, but he was always cool with me. He almost got busted once, and I took the fall for him. He said he owed me a favor and he gave me his private number.   I have never taken him up on it. Once I got involved with The Rabbit Hole, they had different ideas.

Terry Price, scientist: Timing is everything. It always has been. Times of tragedy never change that.

Terry Reynolds: Everything got canceled during this crisis, but you know what is never canceled? Laundry.

Miles Lawson: After a period of wondering how we were going to take this to the next phase, we had a breakthrough. One day, we found out that a drug dealer named Jesus had ties to the president. Even better than that, McGee owed Jesus a favor. We'd get Jesus to ask the president to meet him somewhere of our choosing. We'd hide a gun in the bathroom like they did in The Godfather Part 1, so this way when secret service gave him a pat down, they'd see that he was unarmed. He gets up to go to the bathroom and then comes back, aims the gun at everyone. We'd tie them all up and then we'd carry out phase two of our plan, which is to make them admit their crimes so people would finally see the truth.

Jesus Cristos: Me and my big fucking mouth. What do I know about being a resistance fighter, let alone trying to save the world? This is probably the dumbest thing I've ever volunteered for. Remember, I am a drug addict, so I have been in some dangerous situations and have done really stupid things.

James Erickson, crisis manager: I've been coaching Jesus on what to do when he gets everyone in the room. We are going to have our men stationed down the street. At a certain time, we are going to bust in on them. Moments before, he will pull the uzi we've hidden in the bathroom and keep everyone in place. Then we'll tie them up and incarcerate them.

Dolores Pena: A new poll has shown people would rather die than suffer another year of lockdown. There's no cure and prospects of life ever returning to normal seem more and more bleak each day. In other news, it's supposed to rain for 5 days in a row.

Jesus Cristos: When I reached out to the president, I wasn't sure if he would remember me, let alone take my call. But he did. We caught up briefly. I congratulated him on his rise from crappy senator to President of the United

States. I asked him if he'd ever seen The Godfather and he said he didn't watch mafia movies because they were too personal. He was glad to hear from me because he wanted to see if I could hook him up with some stuff. Obviously, the pressure was unlike anything he'd ever experienced before, so he was looking to relieve some stress.

Ash Gray, secret service: McGee gave us the night off because he wanted private time to meet up with an old friend. He insisted and we argued. We agreed that instead of the normal six guards, there would just be two. A lot of people hate him and I am one of those people, but I am not letting him get assassinated on my watch!

Basil McGee: I promised my guys I quit drugs when I became Vice President. They are going to give me the world's biggest lecture when they find out I am using drugs again. I can't fire them because they really have my back. A lot of people want to stick knives in it. Since I am in charge, if they don't do everything I say, I'll sack those bastards. Who's going to hire them now? There are no jobs anymore.

Jesus Cristos: I couldn't sleep for days. I knew that if anything went wrong, I'd probably be killed or put in prison for the rest of my life. This was not going to be like any other drug deal I've ever done. The first rule of dealing is never do any of your stash. I was so scared, I violated the cardinal rule.

Art Myers: Every time progress is made, there is always something to fuck it up. It's happened all throughout history. Here we are on the edge of a positive change and we put it in the hands of a drug dealer. People think my ideas about things are nuts. Well, I am going out on a limb and saying the future of humankind is really doomed.

Al Lee, spiritual guru: When you've got something to lose, you recoil from strife. When you've got nothing to lose, you fight back.

Miles Lawson: At the agreed upon time, we showed up at the restaurant and Jesus was standing outside with the most bewildered look on his face.

Jesus Cristos: President McGee with his two secret service guys showed up at the agreed upon time. They frisked me and we went inside.   There was a little bit of small talk exchanged and we were getting ready to make our deal. I took a big hit in the bathroom. As we had planned, there was an uzi in the toilet tank. When I came back from the bathroom, I was pointing it at the president and his two guards. They saw me and they told me to drop the gun or they would shoot.   I panicked.   Everyone fired their weapons at the same time. I blew the three of them away. I have a gaping wound in my stomach.

Miles Lawson: Jesus was not saying anything. He was white as a ghost. He started foaming at the mouth. He dropped to the ground and uttered his final words – "Got 'em." Jesus was a martyr. Jesus died for our sins. Praise Jesus!

Dolores Pena: Breaking news! President Basil McGee has been assassinated. Details are still coming in, but we've gotten a report that a man called Jesus has killed the president. More details will be reported soon. Stay tuned.

Chapter 8: Utopia

Miles Lawson, dentist: Citizens of the world: we've been lied to, cheated, oppressed.   ACPh6.9 has been made worse because of the mismanagement by the very people that were supposed to protect us. Their evil reign is over. If you've had any doubts about why this needed to happen, think about your life over the last two years. You haven't had one. All we've had are restrictions and lies. They've done everything they can to keep us uneducated about the truth. Please consider this. If we all stop following their oppression, we will be free.   Now that the president is out of the way, the rest of the battle can be peaceful. All you have to do is repeat these words: We are not going to take it anymore. Break the shackles. Come outside and shout this out – "We are free!"

Dolores Pena, mainstream media: We are getting reports that people everywhere are in the streets, peacefully chanting – "We are free!"   Although there is no cure for ACPh6.9, it appears that lockdown is finally over.

Tim Francis, priest: I told you that Jesus would save us all! We are saved!

Miles Lawson: This escalated quickly. Faster than we could have ever imagined. We are making things up as we go on the fly, but what we do know is that the people have had enough and we've entered into a new world. This world is going to replace the lies and repression with love, togetherness and understanding. For this to work, we need 100% participation.

Devin Silver, novelist: I've got it! I will write about the oppression of the people in the old world. How they were lied to all these years and how once they've opened their eyes and eliminated the real enemy, peace has finally come to the people.

Terry Reynolds, pandemic comedian: What do you get when you kill the very thing that has oppressed you? Freedom. Not one of my funnier bits, I know.

Miles Lawson: It's so interesting how no one seems to be afraid of ACPh6.9 anymore. Sure, it's still a threat, but without the constant state of fear they've been subjecting us to, life seems infinitely better.

Dolores Pena: Now the lockdown is over, things are far from being back to normal. There is a noticeable difference, however. Everyone is acting in an orderly fashion, people are much kinder to each other and there is no more violence on the streets.

Art Myers, conspiracy theorist: A set of guidelines must be distributed at once to the people because otherwise, human nature is going to rear its ugly head and then we are going to be back to the way we were. It probably will go back that way regardless. If we've learned nothing over the past several hundred years, it's that people are their own worst enemy.

Miles Lawson: We've kept a running list of things that have been taken away from us or suppressed for all this time.

We want them returned to the people immediately. We will be holding a public town hall where we hammer out the most important needs of the people.

Alex Schilling, concerned citizen: We need universal health care for all.

Janis Duran, concerned citizen: Why? Lots of countries have it and it doesn't work. How many patients get turned away because there are too many of them and not enough doctors? The situation happening right now is proof of that. Doctors need to make a living too.

Juliette Block, town hall counsel: Doctors will be compensated fairly so they can provide for their families. Services will be provided on a first come, first served basis. No one will get preferential treatment. There will be a special unit for emergencies and a special unit for elective procedures such as plastic surgery.

Jackie Conger, concerned citizen: No more payments from civilians to the government. Make them raise money the old-fashioned way – by pounding the pavement like we have to do. We pay taxes to keep them running and for what? So they can impose new laws, bail out massive corporations, not make us feel any safer, lie to us constantly and when they finally try to help us financially with stimulus checks, they are less than our rent costs!

Sonny Marks, concerned citizen: How do we know if these are lies? Everyone is after power.   It's a matter of who do we trust? But how do we know who to trust? Money and power make people do crazy things. It's always been like that.

Juliette Block: We've established a council of diverse citizens. People will vote on which things are working and which ones are not. It will be majority rules. It's the only fair way. If everyone does not participate, you are not being a rebel. You are surrendering. There will be a maximum wage imposed so people cannot hoard money.

After you reach a certain limit, you will give that money to a special fund which will be distributed to people in need. You will no longer be allowed to pass on your riches to your descendants. No more nepotism. As far as we know, there might not be any offspring to pass it to anyway since a lot of our children are dead and most people are infertile.

Ivy Stack, concerned citizen: What about freedom of religion?

Donna Ward, concerned citizen: Spirituality does not need religion. Religion needs spirituality.

Juliette Block: Believe what you want, but if you force it on someone else, there needs to be a punishment. Get off the cross! We need the wood. No one is going to die because they believe in something different than you. When we were quarantined, no one was "chosen" based on their religion. The virus has killed men, women, people of all races, ideologies and sexual preferences. Therefore, it has

been proven that we are all the same. We are one race –
human. Let's start acting like it.

Roslyn Clemens, concerned citizen: Should we all have one currency?

Walt Baker, concerned citizen: Money is the root of all evil. With all this stuff shut down, we can see this to be true. There has to be a better way.

Juliette Block: If the currency plan outlined earlier does not work, there will be a system of credits. Do something good for the betterment of humankind, receive a credit. Do something that harms us, a credit will be taken away. We are not looking to punish people. We are trying to stop selfish people from ruining life for others. For example, with drugs – if you want to take drugs and ruin your own life, that's great. Go for it. We want people to have more freedom, not be less free.

Miles Lawson: Let's really practice the most important things of religious texts – do unto others as you would have them do unto you. Love thy neighbor – the rest is commentary. All you need is love. We realize this sounds like cheesy social media spirituality, but if you think about it, what more do you really need? Love for each other.

Marty Clark, concerned citizen: What about free housing?

Sherilyn Eaton, concerned citizen: Yeah, like are celebrities supposed to move out of their mansions into smaller places and live with the common people?

Juliette Block: It may sound unfair at present moment to not honor the achievements that people had in the past, but that was then and this is now. The old world does not exist anymore and it did not work for the greater good. Now we live in a world of equality. We have not arrived yet, but we will get there. An item of priority is to build housing that is the same for everyone. People selfishly taking priority over others is one of the reasons we ended up in this mess. Those days are over.

Wally Berg, concerned citizen: It's great there is no war, but what about prisons?

Juliette Block: This is true. We want peace. We can only achieve it if we all work together. This is the first time in history where people are on the same page. We are not going to allow anyone or anything to disturb it. Destroying the peace is a punishable offense.   Like in the old world, going to prison will be a decision that is entirely yours.   If you don't want to go, don't exhibit behavior that will put you and all of us at risk. Life is no longer about you. Instead it's about us. There is no "I" in team, but there is a "you" in "you better not be a selfish asshole."

Vicky Chance, concerned citizen: What about ACPh6.9?

Juliette Block: It's still a danger and we should continue to practice safety measures, but we have to move on with our lives. The communicability rate did not match the lockdown measures they gave us. The original endgame of ACPh6.9 was to make us turn on each other, crush the economy and to keep us controlled. All of those things were achieved. Remember, the news is not called "the facts." They report what they deem worthy of "news." There's a huge difference. Remember, they had an agenda to carry out. That agenda was not in the best interests of the people. Negativity sells.

Miles Lawson: We uncovered useless industries. Now we are going to have to pivot and people are going to have to do things they may not have wanted to do. We need people to help the food supply chain so we can build up our reserve again as it was destroyed when we were in lockdown. A list of industries that no longer serve a purpose includes, but should not be limited to – politicians, news reporters, lawyers, financial professionals, sports, the hospitality industry and celebrities. We are all going to have to be entertainers. We are all going to have to be teachers. We are all going to have to be farmers and builders. No one will be getting awards. Don't martyr yourselves. We have more important things to do.

Teresa Barrow, concerned citizen: Prejudice?

Juliette Block: We must all do our best to ensure the safety and general welfare of all our citizens. We must help those in need such as the elderly, the disabled or pregnant women. It does not look like people are able to reproduce at the moment, but we hope that will eventually be the case again. All citizens need to be treated without prejudice and fear. If there is equality for all, we will be safe. Unless the circle remains unbroken, there will be danger. We've tried every other way of living from communism to fascism to capitalism. It only benefits the top portion of the pyramid. Let's try a new way that benefits the entire pyramid.

Ruth Jenkins, concerned citizen: Will there be one universal language?

Juliette Block: People have religious freedom and can speak whatever language they desire. We just ask that when in public spaces, everyone tries to not get argumentative over these issues or act like their traditions are better than someone else's. The whole purpose of this exercise is for us all to be equal. I hope people can understand this and be at peace with it.

Terry Reynolds: People have been telling me to go plow a field for years. With all the recent events, I have become officially unemployed. The good news is, I can now go plow a field. I'll be helping people too!

Dolores Pena: This will be our final broadcast. This is it. The series finale of the news. We had a good run. I will go to my grave with the knowledge that I did my best to provide a quality product for the people.   I had no knowledge of the endgame. My bosses gave me the script to read to you night after night. I was just carrying out orders. If it makes me a horrible human being, then I will just have to live with it.

Craig Barlow, family man: Ever since the lockdown started, my family and I were at each other's throats. I joked that if the virus didn't kill them, I might. We were just scared and nervous so unfortunately, we took out these fears on each other. But now, it's like the pressure suddenly lifted and we get along great. We sing songs, tell each other jokes and reminisce about stories from our past.

Phoebe Little, celebrity: It's a little strange going from a 10-bedroom mansion to a one room cell, but I was outvoted. I have no choice. I will continue to say until my dying day that this is unfair, but I don't think it's worth it to start a revolt. Besides, if I tried, I'd probably be arrested.

Virgil Moss, psychic: I see this working for a while, but ultimately, human nature is a monster that is very hard to defeat. Just like The Rabbit Hole was formed in secret, we can presume a Utopian takedown group is probably forming right now as well. What could their goal be? Dystopia? I don't know. I am looking into this, but I keep getting distracted as I am obligated to work in the fields.

Aaron Evans, conservative citizen: This is far from ideal in the eyes of the conservatives because so many of us who should be at a higher financial bracket are on the same level as those who did not work as hard as us. They didn't save as much as we did and didn't contribute as much to society as us and we're all equal. That seems like inequality to me.

Lester Orchard, liberal citizen: I always found myself to be an extremist, and in my wildest dreams, I never imagined something as extreme as this. But I'm here for it!

Miles Lawson: Things are working! I hope people realize we are groping in the dark. This has never been done before and we are doing the best we can to make sure the needs of everyone are met. People should expect that there will be bumps in the road from time to time. Certain things are going to fail and fail miserably. The beauty is we are doing everything with love, tolerance and understanding. That is the only way forward. Even the doubters are seeing that while this new world is not perfect, it's better than anything we've ever experienced before.

Brian Powell, alien researcher: All the work I've done is for nothing. I am not allowed to work full time to continue my life's mission. I felt we were so close to finding the answers to the questions we had about life on other planets and in the solar system. But with having to work all day in the fields, how am I supposed to have the time or energy to continue my research? I want to protest, but no one cares.

Trent Harlan, prison warden: Before you jump down my back about holding people in prison cells, I just want to let you know we have specific guidelines from the council about what is and what is not acceptable behavior. Obviously, the people from the old world who committed crimes have been interviewed. If they are still not showing remorse, we cannot let them back out onto the streets. Without them posing a danger to society, we are able to move forward for the safety and betterment of the population at large.

Devin Silver: I am not even mad that I am no longer allowed to work full time on my great American novel. I was still not confident about the story line anyway. I wish I wasn't so wishy washy.

Cara Wilkerson, hospital chief of staff: The death count has finally started to slow down. Suicides are down as people no longer feel life is hopeless. This is great news. As far as the virus goes, the number of new cases of ACPh6.9 is also starting to slow, but we still want to reiterate that there is no cure, no vaccine and it could flare up again at any time.

Billy Weaver, factory worker: It's amazing we have so much help now. During the heart of this crisis, we were working ourselves to the bone. Couldn't even take a bathroom break. You probably don't want to know how many cans of corn I had to pee into over the years. We sold them too, but that's a side story for another day. Thankfully, those days are gone. Now we can actually take breaks and we are helping the world by making sure the food supply chain continues. I feel a little bad for some of these privileged people from the old world like CEOs who think working in a factory is below them. We all have to eat, don't we? If they try to boss me around, I let them know I will turn them in if they continue their crap and that sets them straight. They never give me attitude again when they realize they could be spending the rest of their lives in prison, and not even for committing a crime. It's a win-win as far as I am concerned.

Roxanne Walker, formerly homeless: Before the new world, I was living on the streets. Sometimes I didn't eat for weeks. Other times, I had to eat rats.   In the wintertime, I was freezing because I had nowhere to live. Now I've got my own little place. I have a job and I live next to all these people who used to have interesting lives. I get to hear their great stories. They bitch and moan that they hate living around poor people, so I just keep my mouth shut and tell them I don't like to talk about the past.

Elizabeth Burke, former politician: I used to make laws, now I have to follow them. If I get into trouble, I can't call in any favors and get preferential treatment. I don't like this and I am sure it's all going to come crumbling down. I loved to create problems and then solve them. It always made me look like a hero. Now I'm just average. It doesn't benefit me or anyone else if I work hard or if I just half-ass it. Eventually, this whole system we have will fail.

Victor Carter, former stockbroker: When I was on top of the world, I had the power to make someone a superstar or bring them to their knees. Now people barter for things. It's very hard to accept. There are times where I didn't produce enough, and I get a smaller portion than others. This has taken a lot to adjust to, but if it continues, I will probably commit suicide. This kind of life is not for me.

Richard Berry, doctor: Whatever the former government put in that hand sanitizer they gave to us, it made everyone I've tested sterile. What are we going to do about continuing humanity after our generation dies? All the children are dead and none of us are getting any younger. I can't help but think this was all part of some greater master plan they never let us in on. It's tragic the world has finally gotten its act together and there's not going to be another generation to enjoy the fruits of our labor that has taken literally centuries to achieve.

Jimmy Rios, former mainstream media: It's so weird to not put on a suit each day and read the news to people. Also, I thought these so-called Utopians were supposed to be nice to everyone, but I get dirty looks or nasty comments everywhere I go because of my past job. Bunch of hypocrites. How is this supposed to work if people are just faking it. How can a system that was built on quicksand sustain itself?

Harvey Fink, former con artist: In the old world, I was a scammer. Fake stocks, fake art, and anything I could do to con people out of money. There was no one better than me. I've had no choice since things changed and I've gone legitimate. It's unfortunate because people are more vulnerable than ever. They believe everything. I think the council telling everyone how we should live is a bigger con than any I've pulled off, but there's no one to talk to about this.   I don't want to risk going to a holding cell because there is no innocent until proven guilty anymore. Some people call it Utopia, I call it totalitarianism.

Maggie Chan, heiress: I probably have the worst luck in the world! I was married to this old creep for a long time because I was going to inherit his entire fortune. It was a lot. I put up with so much shit over the years. Every time he was sick and about to die, somehow, he came back stronger than ever. So I waited. And waited. He was verbally and physically abusive. I knew if I just made it through, my life would be amazing. He finally passed away right before the world changed. I was all set for a huge pay day. Now they tell me, I must be like everyone else. I don't see what the point of living is anymore.

Lee Galvin, former CEO: I've run many businesses in my life. Some succeeded beyond my wildest dreams and others failed miserably. You don't have to be a scientist, not that you could be one in this new society anyway, to figure out this is not going to work. Life is like a pyramid. The top of the pyramid have all the power. The middle section are hopeful they can get to the top – some will, most won't, but that's the dream they chase after. The bottom level are the workers that will never even ascend to the middle level, let alone the top. The people in the middle are trying to keep the bottom level from rising but will never rise themselves. We are now all on the bottom and the so-called council is all on top. Eventually, people will catch on and there's going to be a power struggle. How could there not be? Human nature is what it is.

Chapter 9: Utopia Falls

5 years later

Miles Lawson, dentist and council member: They said it could never happen. They said it would never work. Without the news and evil agencies trying to scare the shit out of the public, we have seen that the concept of Utopia does work! Perhaps that was their plan all along? Keep everyone confused and angry so we fall in line with their wishes. We have some folks who are still bitter they are being treated the same as everyone else, as they feel more entitled than others. We had to lock them away for everyone's safety.

Ozzie Madden, former billionaire and philanthropist: No thanks to the Council, I have been working my ass off trying to find a vaccine for ACPh6.9. I haven't been sleeping and I've been stressed out to the max. I believe we should all have the opportunity to live in a world where we can go outside and not be worried about catching ACPh6.9.

Others may not be explicitly saying it, but I know it's what everyone wants. It's certainly what I want.

Miles Lawson: I don't trust Ozzie Madden. He makes it sound like he is not making this for everyone's best interest. You can sense his bitterness towards the council. He's not even trying to conceal it. It's hiding in plain sight. I am not sure how others cannot see it. I am going on record and letting it be known I don't trust him.

Dennis Gray, concerned citizen: I am starting to distrust the council. We've got a guy who is trying to make a vaccine for all of us and they are trying to stop him. Is this a competition to see who has the bigger dick? Maybe. I don't even care. What I do care about is my safety and the safety of my family. I am not sure if the council has my best interests at heart. I am very disappointed.

Rose Evans, concerned citizen: Don't you see? This is how societies fail. You get them to start dissenting. What works for one group of people, doesn't work for the other group.

That's the way it has always been, but once you start with the accusations, people get so angry. The next thing you know, the truth becomes irrelevant. They are too focused on being mad to think calmly and rationally.

Art Myers, conspiracy theorist: Here it comes. From out of the shadows, evil steps into the light. The curtain is being pulled back. Sides are going to be chosen. The war is not over. It's just beginning.

Ruby Hamilton, pro-vaccine: Anyone standing in the way of this vaccine is the enemy. We've been living in fear for 7 years and we are finally on the precipice of safety. If we don't get 100% buy in from everyone, there are going to be the sick mixing with the healthy and then we are all unsafe. That makes no sense.

Eric McIntosh, anti-vaxxer: The person making this is not trustworthy. He's not getting his evil vaccine into my body. Look him up. He's run failed businesses in the past that crippled people financially and surprise surprise, he got very rich off it. He's not in this for the greater good. He's in this for himself, like he's always been. He was working with President Goodman and we know how that played out. If we trust him, I assure you he will betray us.

Ozzie Madden: I am fully aware of the smear campaign being launched against me. I would not have gotten as far as I did in the old world without researching all the facts and all the possibilities. What I can tell you is that the accusations against me are false. What you must ask yourself is what does the council have to gain from suppressing me? The answer – control. They will start taking away your rights little by little until it's a dictatorship. Think about all the people who had to make a major reduction in living. Think about the people who upgraded their lives as a result of the new world. It's disproportionate. Connect the dots for yourself and you will see they don't add up!

Billy Weaver, factory worker: I think we need this vaccine. This is just going to keep passing itself around if we are all not immune to it. Yes, I realize the numbers of infections and deaths have gone way down. The so-called curve has flattened. Big deal. I don't know what I can do to make everyone in my factories see this. Each day is now turning into a debate and people are starting to not want to work together for the common good. If we don't all reach an agreement, there is going to be a slowdown in the supply chain. We saw a few years ago what happened. It resulted in chaos on the streets. God damn it! We've worked so hard to get to this moment and it's all about to be flushed down the toilet because no one can agree.

Tim Francis, priest: Jesus saved us once. He can save us again. We have got to all come together. We must put aside our differences and agree that the vaccine is the most important thing.   Until we have complete control of ACPh6.9, we are going to be tormented.

Walt Baker, concerned citizen: We are never in control of our lives. We never were and never will be. It's all an illusion. We've created fake bullshit like "time" in efforts to give us some semblance that we're in control. We pacify our egos with things like "happiness" and "sadness" but that's to stop us all from going mad when we realize we have no control over anything. We don't know when we are going to die, whether our girlfriends or boyfriends are going to fuck us or where our next meal is going to come from. Things have gotten a little bit better ever since the new world came about, but here we are again getting at each other's throats. And over what? Power? Control? This story is so old! They say if we don't learn from the past and history, we are doomed to repeat it. Look what just happened! Hello! Is there anyone out there?

Holly Paulson, liquor store clerk: The drinking rate is starting to go up again. Haven't seen it like this since the old world where people were drinking themselves to death because of the fallout from ACPh6.9. I've been hearing yelling in the streets. People are being divided into two camps: the ones in favor of the vaccine and those against it.

Bobbie Starr, former pornography actress: It's my body. I will put in it what I want to. Yes, the argument is that in the past, it's semi well known I sucked a lot of dicks and swallowed, but that was then and this is now. Since the new world began, I have not had any alcohol, no drugs and certainly no cocks! I am just a non-preachy, Jesus loving farm girl, living a healthy life.

Ozzie Madden: The vaccine is almost ready. We're all going to be free once we take it. We just need to get through it. It's just a little pin prick. There'll be no more virus. We will start working on the cure for sterility after everyone takes the vaccine. Once we have that, life can resume as normal. Here's the thing, nothing is perfect, and I must have total control over the distribution of my drug so we can all be safe. As you can see from the actions of the council, they are trying to take me down. I cannot and will not trust them to do the right thing. Furthermore, I will accept no responsibility if anything goes wrong from taking it.

Miles Lawson: He's starting to show his true colors. He wants total authority but will be taking no blame. I have to admit, it's a very interesting leadership philosophy. Granted it sounds a little psychopathic.

Cory Bowers, ACPh6.9 survivor: I will be first in line to try it. We live in a world where there is no fame, so this could be my little moment in the sun. Where do I sign up? People have said to me, "What if it kills you?" Come on! I have survived ACPh6.9 and I don't ever want to get it again or even risk it. It was the worst feeling of my life. So painful. I thought I'd never fuck again. Now I have come back from that, we need to make sure everyone has access to this vaccine.

Ozzie Madden: I am getting sick and tired of people doubting this. It's exhausting. I am trying to make the world a better place and all I am getting from all sides is shit being thrown at me. They are trying to drag my name through the mud. They are calling me childish names. They are doubting my product and now people don't even want to take it, which is only going to put us all in danger. They say I have an end game in all this. Let me repeat this: there is no end game. I am not trying to put microchips in people so I can control their minds and stop people from having human emotion. However, I must admit, that sounds like a genius plan. This is the biggest conspiracy theory ever concocted.

Miles Lawson: People! Wake up. He admitted his plan in his own words and it came straight out of his own mouth. How can you not see this? We worked so hard to get here and things have been working out so great. It's all going to be for nothing if we don't act and act right now. Please. I beg you. Do not listen to that man. He's playing you for fools!

Ozzie Madden: I am fed up with this. It was not enough that I was giving this away for free to everyone. But now, it's going to cost you. I will only provide this vaccine if the council dissolves. I will install my own team to oversee the vaccine process and those clowns that are on the council will be out on their asses and maybe even incarcerated. Period! These are my terms. Take them or leave them.

Cara Wilkerson, hospital chief of staff: Here we go again. Suicide rates are going up once more. This is like the never-ending yo-yo. As a medical professional, I can honestly say I have had enough of this. For years, my emotions have been thrown around like a ball. As soon as it seems hopeful, there is darkness. Once everything becomes dark, there is a glimmer of light. I don't care anymore. Give us the vaccine or don't, but can we just make a decision and get it over with already?!

Juliette Block, council member: This is so depressing. We are watching the best society we've ever had in our lifetime wither away and die. It's slipping right through our fingers.

Tim Francis: God wants us to have this vaccine. He wants us to be able to procreate again. It's the whole point of life. These sinners out there that don't want to get a vaccine are ruining the world for all of us that want to let it continue. We have prayed and this is the way forward.

Juliette Block: We will put it to a vote. It's the only fair thing to do in this Utopian society. We beg and plead to please come to your senses, but at the same time, we know this society only works if we take everyone's needs into consideration.   Just remember that once he has control, it's not reversable and there is no telling what he might do.

Nancy Yeager, concerned citizen: Why do people not trust this guy? He's admitted he's not perfect. He's admitted he has heard all the nasty things people have said about him and he still holds his head up high. That's pretty admirable. Most people in positions of power try to deny everything and act like they are perfect. I think we should give him a chance.

Dennis Gray, concerned citizen: Are people crazy? He's a wolf in sheep's clothing. He will say or do anything to make us gain his trust and by the time the masses see his true colors, it will be too late.

Ozzie Madden: I would just like to make one final statement before the voting tomorrow. Please consider this – the council have brainwashed you into thinking that there is no need for a vaccine, but let me just remind you once more that people are still dying from ACPh6.9 and human sterilization is real. Do you want to die? Do you want your family lineage to carry on? Do you want the council to stop you from reaching your full, unlimited potential? If the answer to at least one of those questions is yes, please vote for the vaccine.

Juliette Block: We are all for love, peace and understanding. How can people vote yes for this thing? It's not verified. Why don't we test it on him first before we reach our decision? We don't know if it will work and he is trying to destroy the very system we all fought so hard to build. Ask yourselves, has the Utopian society worked for the last five years? Ask yourselves, have you had to starve or worry about having a roof over your head?   Ask yourselves how many people has ACPh6.9 killed recently? Is this worth the risk?   The choice is up to you. We hope you'll vote responsibly. The future is in your hands.

Two days later

Ozzie Madden: The people have spoken and victory is mine. But really, the victory is ours. I will give you the vaccine to defeat ACPh6.9. Once I assemble my team, we will start to work on a way to reverse sterility. You've not just bought yourselves a future, but from now on, from the safety of my mansion, I will make sure the people have what they need. After I take care of my family and my team. It's nothing personal. You agreed to it, fair and square. If anyone tries to get in my way, you will be arrested. What I say goes. There was a huge debate about whether or not you'd have to take the vaccine. The answer is entirely up to you. Don't take it. I really don't care. But if you ever want to eat food again, you will get in line for it. Once you've received the vaccine, which comes with a digital tattoo, you'll be added to the "cleared" list. If your name is not on that list, we will come looking for you. You can run, but you cannot hide forever.

Juliette Block: This is the saddest day of my life. We did everything we could to try and convince the people we were not lying but they didn't listen. Now we are stuck with a dictator, who has the potential to be worse than the last two presidents we had, and everyone knows how awful those two pricks were. As we agreed upon, the council will be dissolved, and Ozzie Madden will install his team. The homeless of the old world will once again be homeless and the rich will presumably be rich again.

Miles Lawson: The greed of mankind knows no bounds. It's a travesty. We never saw the real enemy because we were too busy fighting ourselves and each other. It's our own fault and I don't see any way out of this. To be honest, if life is going to be this crappy, I am not sure it's worth living anymore. I am not suggesting anyone follow my advice. Frankly, I don't care what anyone else does anymore. I just know what I need to do.

Dolores Pena, mainstream media: This is amazing. I got my old job back! I am thrilled. I can once again let the people know the latest. There's probably not going to be anything positive to say for a while, but I am confident that one day, there will be something to smile about again. I will bring you the good with the bad because that's what we on the news do. But first, I will talk about the bad.

Devin Silver, novelist: Now that I've seen how this whole thing has played out, I think I'll drop my idea for a story about a virus and write a romantic comedy instead.

Art Myers, conspiracy theorist: I know this is probably not the most appropriate time to say this, but I told you so.

Epilogue:

1 year later

Ozzie Madden, ruler: Life has returned to the way it should be. The rich on top and the worker bees on the bottom. Life is just too short for us all to be equal. I know it's not fair. Sure the people were a little pissed off at me at first. All they had to do was question everything and conduct their own research, but it didn't happen and here we are. Once they got their vaccine, they were happy. Those microchips that were implanted into people hardly gave anyone discomfort. To those who think I am a bad guy, look what I did for humanity. Now the world is totally free from ACPh6.9!

Juliette Block, former council member: My brain is no longer my own. I feel devoid of all human emotion. I don't care what happens anymore. I will do whatever they ask as long as I get my yearly injection upgrade. I need it!

Dolores Pena, mainstream media: You'll never know the goodness of sweet until you've tasted sour. Supreme Leader Madden has finally revealed his end game, but it's too late to stop him. The microchips in the ACPh6.9 vaccine are controllable. Before people have a chance to revolt or cause upset, he puts a stop to it by remote.

Ozzie Madden: I knew once people gave it a chance, they would agree that the world is safer. I will try not to abuse my power, but the world is a dangerous place, so that is really a promise I cannot make. Now let us rejoice in a world free of ACPh6.9 once and for all.

Gavin Scott, homosexual: I'm a gay guy who has been paranoid about all this vaccine stuff. It sounded like gay conversion therapy to me. Throughout history, even in the best of times, my people have been oppressed. When this so-called Utopian society started, I decided to go off the grid with my bestie, Jane Greenblatt. We've hidden out under the radar all this time. Sometimes we found food, other times, we starved. Even though we were not sexually compatible, people have needs. I accidentally got her pregnant a few times over the years, but we always aborted. We've heard that humanity is in grave danger of ending due to everyone being sterile. We talked about having a child to potentially continue the human lineage, but the more we thought about it, we decided that no child should have to put up with the bullshit that the human race has to offer. The greed. The jealousy. The competition. So we are just going to hide out here until we hear the footsteps of Ozzie Madden's thugs. When that day comes, we have lethal doses of drugs we will shove into our veins. This is their problem, not ours.

1 week later

Dolores Pena: We are getting reports that multiple people in various cities have died from a new virus that is sweeping through the nation. We can confirm from the autopsies that the virus these people died from is not ACPh6.9. At this time, there is no vaccine.

Terry Reynolds, pandemic comedian: What do you call a population that only cares about itself and will destroy anything and everything that gets in its way, often punishing itself at the same time? A plague.

The End

<u>Also by Geoffrey Dicker</u>

Sketches of Verbal Alchemy

Unfinished Lyrics

I Won The Internet – Daily Wit, Wisdom and Selfies, According to G

Journal of Grievances

Twisted Tales and Very Short Stories

Goddamned! - A Play

Post Celebrity

Paddling Backwards

In Bad Company (Coming Soon)

About the Author

Geoffrey Dicker is the author of 10 books including "Sketches of Verbal Alchemy," a controversial collection of 'abstract poetry.' "Unfinished Lyrics," is an anthology of song lyrics he's written. Three full length albums of his words have been recorded by singer Jim Emmons ("In the Absence of Red," "Throwing Stars" and "So Strange"). The song "Manhunt," performed by Jeremy Gloff, was featured in the film "Eating Out: The Open Weekend." "I Won the Internet!" Dicker's 3rd book, features wit, wisdom and celebrity selfies. "Journal of Grievances," his first novel, is a raw and uncensored look into the ups and downs (both in and out of the bedroom) of a struggling, single gay male writer in New York about to turn 40. "Twisted Tales and Very Short Stories," is a collection of 200 stories that are each shorter than one page. "Goddamned," which was released in 2018, is his first play. "Post Celebrity" is a dark comedy set in the future, told in short stories. "Paddling Backwards," a novel, is a supernatural love story. His art and music blog According2g.com ran over 6,000 posts that featured his world exclusive photos over the course of 5 years. Simultaneously, he amassed over 3.8 million views on his live concert video YouTube channel. He has taken more than 2,000 selfies with famous people and has amassed more than 25,000 autographs in his personal collection. Geoffrey Dicker has lived in Los Angeles, New York and currently resides in Chicago.

Follow him on: Twitter or Instagram @according2g

www.ingramcontent.com/pod-product-compliance
Lightning Source LLC
Chambersburg PA
CBHW071937150726
47999CB00001B/233